in deep

Also by Terra Elan McVoy

Pure

After the Kiss

The Summer of Firsts and Lasts

Being Friends with Boys

Criminal

in deep

TERRA ELAN MCVOY

Simon Pulse

NEW YORK • LONDON • TORONTO • SYDNEY • NEW DELHI

This book is a work of fiction. Any references to historical events, real people, or real places are used fictitiously. Other names, characters, places, and events are products of the author's imagination, and any resemblance to actual events or places or persons, living or dead, is entirely coincidental.

SIMON PULSE

An imprint of Simon & Schuster Children's Publishing Division
1230 Avenue of the Americas, New York, NY 10020
First Simon Pulse hardcover edition July 2014
Copyright © 2014 by Terra Elan McVoy

SIMON PULSE and colophon are registered trademarks of Simon & Schuster, Inc.
For information about special discounts for bulk purchases, please contact Simon &
Schuster Special Sales at 1-866-506-1949 or business@simonandschuster.com.
The Simon & Schuster Speakers Bureau can bring authors to your live event.
For more information or to book an event contact the Simon & Schuster Speakers
Bureau at 1-866-248-3049 or visit our website at www.simonspeakers.com.
Cover design by Regina Flath
Interior design by Hilary Zarycky
The text of this book was set in Electra.
Manufactured in the United States of America
2 4 6 8 10 9 7 5 3 1
Library of Congress Cataloging-in-Publication Data
McVoy, Terra Elan.
In deep / Terra Elan McVoy. — First Simon Pulse hardcover edition. pages cm
Companion book to: The summer of firsts and lasts. Summary: "A competitive
swimmer gets in over her head as she plays a wicked cat-and-mouse game with her
wild best friend and a hot new college swimmer"— Provided by publisher.
[1. Best friends–Fiction. 2. Friendship—Fiction. 3. Competition (Psychology)–
Fiction. 4. Swimming–Fiction.] I. Title. PZ7.M478843In 2014 [Fic]—dc23
2013045350
ISBN 978-1-4814-0136-4
ISBN 978-1-4814-0138-8 (eBook)

To Meg,

who asked if there was more about this Brynn character

GRIER AND I ARE FLOATING IN HER GLOSSY, TURQUOISE POOL, both of us in separate inner tubes, pushing each other around with our feet and staring at the dark, humid sky when she goes, "Dare me to do something."

I raise my head to look at her. Sure, she had suck times at the meet today, and pizza with the team afterward is always a Michael Phelps–praising bore, but we haven't played Dare in a while. Mainly because at this point we can't think of anything we haven't already done that isn't completely disgusting, would require too much pain-in-the-ass planning or equipment, or would end up with one of us getting seriously hurt or arrested. That I got tired of her chickening out one too many times was part of it too, which is why I'm surprised now. And, I'm out of practice.

"Uh—I dare you to pretend you're in love with Shyrah for a week."

She groans. "Way too easy."

Which is true. If one of the other girls in the club even looks at Shyrah for too long at practice, he's sneaking up to me later, asking me should he ask her out.

"Okay. I dare you to . . ." I look around, trying to find something. We already climbed on top of the cabana once, to see if we could jump from there into the pool, but the distance really is too far. "I dare you to lick Peebo's butthole."

She grins and starts whistling for her dog.

"Sick." I splash her. "I was just kidding. He's inside, anyway."

"Here," she says, slipping free of her tube. I watch her slide underwater to the ladder, where she climbs out, tugging the edges of her bikini away from her narrow butt. I've seen Grier's body a thousand times, but it doesn't make her elfish perfectness any less obvious. Other girls on the team are jealous, I guess. Maybe I would be too if she weren't so slow in the water. She even looks good with her head shaved now, after I *Jackass*ed her with a pair of clippers last month and took a huge hunk right out of her dark, glossy locks. Her mom was plenty pissed, but even Grier thought it was funny, and now she just looks sexier. More tough.

She moseys over to the cabana and starts rummaging behind

the bar. I don't really feel like drinking tonight, but at Grier's it's always around. Daring her to drink some kind of crazy mixed-up shot isn't much of a dare anymore either, but maybe this will make her less pissy or whatever it is she's been lately.

Not that Grier is that complicated. I met her when I left my high school team to join our more challenging private swim club at the end of ninth grade. Grier's a sprinter (I'm long-distance), and she'd already been a member of the club for two years, so she seemed dedicated, like me. Over time, though, she revealed herself to be the kind of girl I didn't think existed in real life. That gorgeous rich girl with an absent, globe-trotting father and a pill-addled, socialite mother; the girl who gets to spend three hundred dollars at Whole Foods on her parents' credit card over the weekend because that's easier than either of them having to figure out how to actually take care of her. She's that girl who vacations in Bali or the cliffs of Iceland or some other no-high-schooler-really-visits-there place. She goes to the best private school in Atlanta, and still her parents are constantly talking about sending her to London because they don't think she's getting an adequate education here. (Grier says they just want her out of their hair once and for all, but she'd still love to go.) She swims, mainly, so she can gorge on gourmet pizzas, organic hamburgers, bottomless margaritas, and expensive desserts. In middle school, whenever I read books that had characters like Grier in them, I'd say, "Nobody's life is really like that."

But that was back when I actually read books. That was before I met Grier.

At first, when she started inviting me over, I thought she was just being nice. It took only two sleepovers though to understand that a rich, pretty girl like her doesn't have to be nice to a scrappy, Salvation Army latchkey kid like me. Instead Grier thought I was funny. Different. She told me once that I'm the only other person who hates people more than she does. And if it works for her, I'm not going to argue.

Now I spend pretty much every weekend over at her place. For me, Grier's the only one in the club who comes close to having a sense of humor or rebellion. Besides, being at her house means I don't have to hang out with Mom and my stepdad, Louis, either. Plus there's the cushy environs and excellent chow. Though Grier and I do the normal things that girls do together—complain, gossip, paint our toenails—we also spend a lot of time watching human stunt videos, which is where Dare came from. I thought I was the only one who was obsessed with "People Are Awesome," and *Jackass*, until I commented under my breath about it at practice, and Grier's eyes lit up like a Christmas tree on fire. We've filled a lot of our weekends with trying to invent stunts of our own—I'm still working on the four-inch-nail-in-the-nose trick—but for the last few weekends, because of what, I don't know exactly, we just watch the videos. And even then she seems bored.

Tonight though, we're apparently back to more than

watching. When Grier comes over to sit on the edge of the pool, she's holding a round container.

"Dare me to snort this salt."

Meaning the margarita salt in her hand.

"That shit's hard little crystals. It'll hurt like hell."

"Yeah, but don't you want to see what happens? There's a sugar rimmer in there too. I'll dare you to do that after."

I don't much want to snort anything, since enough water goes up my nose on a daily basis, but Grier's going to do it whether I dare her or not, and then she'll just call me chicken all night for not making it official. I know. I've done it to her.

"Okay, fine. I dare you to snort that salt."

She takes off the lid and stares into the plastic dish for a moment, and then puts a couple of pinches in a thin line on her wrist. I paddle closer, wanting to see what happens. She waits a beat, holds her wrist up to her nose, and then, whiff, the white line disappears.

"Shit," she says, coughing.

When she looks up, there's blood pouring out her nose.

"Shit," I say back. "Are you okay?"

She coughs again, slightly gagging. "Stings like a bastard."

"Jesus. Let me get you a towel."

I climb out of the water and grab a bath sheet that probably costs more than all the cheap, secondhand furniture in my room combined.

"Wait. Check it out." She points into the pool. Drops of her blood are spiraling and unfurling in the water like devilish smoke. We stare at the blood for what feels like five minutes. Long enough so that the red forms more of a cloud than wisps.

"You need some ice on that." I hand her the towel and stand up for the house.

"Hold up." She leans back toward the lounge chair behind her, reaching for her shorts and her phone. "Take my picture first."

Her chin, throat, and chest are now dripping blood.

"You're not going to post this."

"Why not?" She grins. "At least then we'll have proof something happened, for once. Don't be so boring."

That's a dumb thing to do out of boredom, I almost say. But it'd sound defensive. I need to get her cleaned up anyway, because apparently I'm snorting that sugar next.

It's not like I can let Grier win.

2

SUNDAY'S ALWAYS THE LOWEST POINT OF MY WEEK. THOUGH
sleeping in is great, a day without practice feels a little unhinged,
no matter what else is happening. Grier and I usually make
breakfast, but once she drops me off at home, it's impossible to
avoid Louis and Mom. I end up doing yard work, laundry, or
washing the car. Regular-kid chore things. Sometimes we go on
errands. Or else I just watch TV. Make myself stuff to eat. Go
online, flip through a magazine, or do enough of my homework
to keep up the club's required GPA, which you'd pretty much
have to be in a coma not to get.

The second half of Sunday though—that's when we go to
the cemetery.

My real dad was a firefighter. But he got killed in an accident when I was ten. Lightning hit this elementary school, and a fire started on the roof while some of the administrators were inside, having a work retreat to discuss plans for the new year. The fire spread fast because of the old insulation, plus all the papers in storage. Almost everyone got out, but there were two people in the library who got stuck by a fallen shelf. My dad and two of his friends rushed in. They got the people out, but then Dad went back for a final check. That's when part of the roof caved in.

They're pretty sure he died right away. That's what my mom told me, anyway. Otherwise he would've lain there, pinned and hurt, feeling the flames close in. I believed her then, and I guess I still do.

I don't remember a lot of the next year. Mom doesn't either, except that I had a lot of nightmares and had trouble getting to sleep at night. We had to move into an apartment. Not a nice one either. I came home from school and stayed there by myself for a few hours until Mom got off of work. Wives of the other guys at the station brought us food for months, which people do when someone dies, I guess, but eventually I realized we wouldn't have eaten at all if they hadn't. I'm not sure what I did with myself when I was on my own. Probably read a lot of books.

Then there was seventh grade, and I must've gotten better because I did have some friends. I got really into scribbling mean parodies of dramas that would happen at school for them, making us all laugh. I guess I was all right.

And then Mom and Louis met at one of their company Christmas parties. They don't work on the same floor or even in the same department, so they hadn't seen each other before, but they didn't waste a lot of time making up for that. We moved again—this time into Louis's house—and I was suddenly in a different school. There was a pool within walking distance. Mom told me I was starting swimming lessons, something we wouldn't have been able to afford even when Dad was alive. It'd get me out of the house, she said. Maybe I could make new friends.

We didn't start going to the cemetery every Sunday until about a year ago. Mom couldn't handle it before, I guess. Or didn't think I could. Maybe she thought Louis would feel strange about it. But on top of being gung ho about becoming the stepdad-slash-swim-cheerleader to the sullen, quiet daughter of a bloated, wrung-out widow, Louis was all on board for making special family time to go visit my dad's grave. I think the whole thing might've even been his idea.

Now my mom has gone gangbusters with it. It's like she needs to show off to Louis how much she cares. Nearly every week we bring something different—fresh flowers or a replacement for the plastic ones she has there in pots. Photos of my dad in cheap frames. Letters she writes to him about me. Pumpkins at Halloween or poinsettias at Christmastime. I only go because they make me. I go because I don't have a choice. But I knew a long time ago that my father wasn't in that hole. When he first died, it felt like maybe his energy was still hovering there, but now when we visit, there's nothing. Just his strong, handsome face in those old, fading photos. My father's not anywhere anymore. Except in whatever scraps that managed to stay distinct after his DNA got all mixed up with Mom's to make me.

TIMOTHY BURRELL POLONOWSKI. BELOVED SON, HUSBAND, AND FATHER. SEPT. 1973–AUG. 2008 the tombstone reads. It always bothers me that he never got to his thirty-fifth birthday. But mainly during our weekly visits I look around at the other graves, the paling flower arrangements. It's quiet here. That is, until another car moves down the long drive, and another family gets out to stand over a piece of grass and a chunk of stone.

Today my mom's actually crying. I clench my quads tight, and squeeze my rib cage toward my bellybutton a few times. Try to exhale in one long stream. Who knows what's gotten into her. Maybe it's because summer's almost here, though still it's three months or something until the anniversary. It's like the cemetery visits have made Mom more goopily nostalgic than she was when he died. Then, she was just—blank. Weak and exhausted all the time, like everything had gotten sucked out of her. There was nothing I could do. Until Louis came along.

"I'm grateful to him," Louis murmurs, rubbing Mom's shoulders. "Every day."

He would squash you, I think. But Louis is being nice. He's taking care of us. Trying to.

So I stand there, arms down by my sides, counting breaths. Eventually we leave. I don't say good-bye, though Mom does, every time.

3

MONDAY MORNING, AS SOON AS THE ALARM BEEPS FROM MY bedside table, my mind is up, knowing what I need to do—mentally packing snacks, pulling on my clothes—but I let myself lie there another ten seconds. Thirty. The idea of thirty more is often tempting, but then the training kicks in and I sit up, put my feet on the floor. Thanks to days and weeks and months of this, it doesn't take much to push myself up and through the steps. Bathroom. Pee. Pajamas off. Pull on any kind of clothes— usually cutoff sweatpants and a long-sleeve T-shirt. Make bed, pound pillow. Accept banana and protein bar from Louis, who is drinking his first cup of coffee. Eat. Pull on ball cap hanging by the door. Grab gear bag as we go out into the garage to get in the car, head to school.

I used to complain, like everybody else. I used to moan. When I first started swimming, I hated it. Hated Louis, in particular, for being so peppy about the whole thing, excited to connect with his new stepdaughter, since he'd never been married and had no kids of his own. The swimming thing was just a random project I guess they both picked for me. But then, sometime in the fall of eighth grade, it became clear to me and everyone else that I was actually good. I could go faster than half my team without even trying. I made Junior Cut before anyone expected.

Somewhere in there I stopped complaining and started appreciating how tough I was getting, how lean and strong I was compared to everyone else. I went through puberty like normal, sure, but with all my swimming, everything on me stayed hard and flat. Other girls started getting boobs and hips, but I was shaped more like a two-by-four than a tart. And the weird thing was, it didn't bother me. It was like my body could do this thing that nobody else's could. I was strong and I was fast. I could hold my breath longer than anyone I knew.

I was also reading and watching a lot of interviews at that time — it's stupid to talk about Lochte or Phelps, but it's stupider not to pay attention to winners like that — and they kept echoing what Van was trying to teach me: That to really succeed, you have to not think about winning or losing. You have to think about nothing at all and just swim. And so then I got this idea in my head to see what, exactly, this body of mine could really do if I got my mind fully out of the way and disciplined myself to do just that. How fast I could go. How far I could swim. How unbeatable I could be.

There were a series of tricks and things I had to use at first— games I'd play with my brain and ways I'd secretly reward or punish myself—but eventually they worked. Now, no matter how tired I am, no matter what's going on, or how tempting another few minutes of sleep might seem, once I get myself up and started, it's like my body just knows what to do.

The best thing is, it always works.

I can't say the same thing for Louis. Unlike me, he needs about three cups of coffee and some kind of sugary carbohydrate before he can function, and every morning it's like he's dragging himself out of the house at 6:45 for the first time. When I get down to the kitchen, he's leaning against the counter and staring into his cup like he can't remember why it's there.

"Louis?"

"Mmph?" Bags under his eyes. Paunch over his belt.

"You ready?" I'm laughing at him. He knows it.

"How many more weeks of this?"

"Five. And then we get to start summer practice." I clap my hands cheerleader-style.

"It's an hour later than all this noise, at least."

I pat him on the shoulder and give him a little shove toward the garage door.

• • •

It's not that he's not into my swimming. Once I joined the club, Louis was more serious about it than I was in some ways. He even changed his work schedule around so he can take me to school, go into work, and then leave an hour earlier than everyone else to take me to practice. The day after my sixteenth birthday, Louis took me for my driver's test, just for safety's sake, but even though we're better off now, we still can't afford another car. This deal works out okay. That there's a Dunkin' Donuts between my school and his office is an added bonus for him, but he really does care. And I know it.

We leave our neighborhood, the radio droning classic rock, though the volume's barely up. As we pull onto Monroe, I point to a dusty maroon station wagon with a low-hanging back end.

"On his way home from a janitorial shift at one of the office complexes downtown."

This is our game. A way to not just sit in the car silently focused on how tired we are or feel like we have to talk about anything else, either. I started it my first summer practice with the club as one of the ways to trick myself. Louis still enjoys it, even during the school year. It's another thing that's comfortingly automatic about my life: playing this game with Louis every morning instead of anything else.

"Which complex downtown?"

"Um . . ." I try to remember any names.

Louis makes the sound of a buzzer and slaps the meaty heel of his hand on the steering wheel. "Too slow, too slow. What about her?"

We're passing the gas station that's a famous hangout for hookers and drug deals.

I make the buzzer noise myself. "Too easy."

"Okay, this guy."

And like that, all the way to school.

4

THAT I DON'T CARE MUCH ABOUT SCHOOL IS AN UNDERSTATE-
ment. But it isn't because I'm so absorbed in my swimming.
(Though that is a mighty convenient justification, for many
teachers.) Instead it's the senseless, mind-numbingness of the
whole situation. The timed bells. The shuffling to the lockers.
The disgusting cafeteria. The way we're all supposed to be so
excited about cheerleading and baseball scores and yearbook
and all that. People say sixteen is the best year of your life — they
make such a stupid deal of it. But sixteen? The pinnacle? Not
for me, thanks. Of course it's true that even the best swimmers
have pretty short careers, but that's why I'm looking for a swim
scholarship to a decent college, away from here. It's not like I
haven't thought this through. Whether my high school peers

know it or not, there needs to be something beyond all this, and for me swimming's the way I'm going to get it.

Maybe it's the classes I'm in—why school mostly sucks. Maybe in AP and IB and Advanced Gifted Superfantastic Film Studies it's all academic overabundant enthusiasm all the time. But I wouldn't know. A lot of the other club members are hard-core students. They do nothing but swim and homework. They obsess about their GPAs, their academic standing, and being in the tenth percentile. Eight hours of sleep a day, and all that. But when I decided to stop thinking and just swim, school fell under the no-thinking umbrella, too. I just didn't see the point. Not here. Not in this place, with its cookie-cutter conversation and overworked, underpaid teachers tiredly reigning over classrooms full of kids whose parents call to hassle them if their precious baby gets less than a B+.

So I don't get to talk about *The Great Gatsby* with Mrs. Bowles and all the lit heads. I don't frown over string theory in Advanced Physics II or whatever, and I don't get to solve the math problems of the universe in Quadruple Trig 1000. Instead I'm as basic as they get: regular English (Mrs. Drummond, who thinks that twenty-first-century high school students are still interested in Newbery Medal–winners from 1964); PE (ha); Math for Dummies (really it's Algebra II with Dr. Herrington, who was cool about it when he failed me last year, and let me take it again instead of doing summer school); Spanish II (easy, because Señora Gupta is half-blind); Enviro Science (with Ms. Chu, who's actually pretty cool); and the one semi-interesting class, Dr. Woodham's U.S. Conflicts, which is just one of the many alterna-history courses this school is famous for offering.

As long as I make it through without fucking up enough to get me thrown out of the club, and as long as I nail National Cut at State next month, it doesn't matter. It's not that I don't want to learn something halfway useful or interesting. It's just that I know I can't do it here. So I get up early and walk through my classes. I don't make myself a disciplinary problem, but I don't really make an effort, either. When the bell rings at the end of the day, I walk out the door and take myself to the pool, which is where I'll earn my way to something better, pretty much anywhere I want.

Having Charlie with me at school has helped—at least, lately. We met on the school team at the start of freshman year and became team pals right away. We rolled our eyes together behind the coach's back, joked around. Buddies, whatever. But I didn't stay on that team long, because, honestly, the team sucks, and I'd heard about the club, which was way more vigorous. Charlie had a girlfriend on the team, this girl Sarah. They were pretty inseparable. After I quit, I didn't see much of him, even though he lives just a couple blocks away. I didn't even know he and Sarah had broken up until Coach Brubeck asked me to go to a meet with them at UGA last month, just to help up their scores and times. On the bus back, tired and pizza-drowsy, Charlie told me all about it—how serious Sarah'd gotten, talking about the future all the time. He said he missed me being around, that the team wasn't the same since I'd left. And I ended up kissing him. I don't know. He's good-looking and funny. A relationship-relationship isn't anything I have time for or interest in, but having someone to get it on with is way better than not, and plus, the extra tiredness after we hang out helps me sleep better.

Today at lunch he's at our table before I am, and as soon as I walk into the cafeteria, he smiles and raises one hand in greeting. I go over, drop my bag in my chair, and head straight for the rack of still-warm plates at the end of the salad bar. Following me in line, he rubs the tight spot between my shoulder blades, but I roll myself out from under his hand, pretending I'm stretching.

"You okay?" I can sense, just by the tone of his voice, that his dark eyebrows are scrunched down.

"I just don't understand why every teacher has to give us a fucking progress report today. PE? Are you serious? Do I care that I have a C in that class? Absolutely not, Coach Bradley. Not in the slightest."

I'm practically flinging banana peppers onto my plate. And, screw—most of the spinach is wet and wilted.

"Month of school left," he says. "Some people want to know."

"Yeah, well, I don't. Just gimme my 2.75 and let me get out of here."

"You worried about Conflicts?"

I ignore him, continuing down the salad bar to the black olives and the feta, mounding my salad high and dousing everything with plenty of oil and vinegar.

"I'm sure it's not as bad as you think," he tries again when we're back at our chairs. "And if it really is, you still have time. The exam's the main thing."

Charlie took U.S. Conflicts last year. This year he's on to Modern Presidential Campaign Strategies or some crap like that. The AP version, I think. If they have that.

"Woodham's not the extra-credit type," I remind him. I know. I asked about it when my third D shook a bit of my confidence about gliding through this class like the others. *Why would I give you extra, Ms. Polonowski,* he'd said, *when it's apparent you're barely interested in getting any credit at all?* Pompous prick-mouth.

Charlie chomps a forkful of red cabbage. There's a glaze of French dressing along the right hump of his upper lip. He talks around it. "Maybe I can help."

"You'll really give me your tests from last year?" I feel halfway hopeful.

He fake-glowers at me. "No. But I can look at yours, give you some pointers, and let you know what to focus on for the next three weeks."

"Jerk."

He pauses, about to put another bunch of cabbage into his mouth, still amused. "You're gonna have to learn sometime, Ivy League."

"You know I don't care about Ivy League."

"Sure you don't."

He's teasing, but it's stupid.

"You may think that the National Merit Scholar Jerkoff Program sounds like fun," I say, "but I'm not interested in spending four years pretending I care about the Pythagorean philosopher's pee hole. Or even discovering nuclear fusion. It just needs to be something besides some Podunk community college around here, is all. I'm not going to turn into my mom."

"Whoa, okay."

I stab my salad. Charlie waits. When he starts up again, instead of being snarky or impatient, he's calm and almost sweet. "No matter where your swimming takes you, you're eventually going to have to study, Polo. Woodham's good practice. And you like that class."

"Woodham's a good asshole is what."

"All you have to do is pass the exam, Brynn. It's not that big a deal."

"I know," I grumble.

"You won't have to go to summer school. Your training will be fine."

I spear the olives and peppers on my plate. I know Charlie

wants me to look at him. I know he wants to try to calm me down, reassure me, or whatever he thinks I need right now. But the only thing that'll make me feel better is getting into the pool and swimming this off. Part of what we're also not talking about here is that since I'm a better swimmer than Charlie is, it's possible I could get into a school that rejects him, even though he makes way better grades. Even if there has to be summer school, which of course there can't be.

"I'll still help you, if you want," he finally says.

"What would really help would be if I could just challenge Woodham to a race. See who's so superior then."

Mainly I say this to take the attention away from Charlie's offer. Though it's nice he wants to help, I can't really picture the two of us, heads together in the library, doing something so boyfriend-girlfriendy. Sitting together at lunch is public enough; I didn't want to do it all, until I realized having someone to complain to, someone in the know about swim difficulties and lingo, helped take the edge off until it was time to be in the pool. For now I shrug without giving him an answer and chew big mouthfuls of my salad.

"A smackdown between you and Woodham would be pretty funny," he says finally. "In fact, I'd pay to see it."

And damn him—in spite of how pissed I am—that does make me laugh.

5

OTHER THAN LUNCH WITH CHARLIE, THE HIGHLIGHT OF MY school day is fifth and sixth periods—two classes back to back with Kate. It's hard to describe who Kate is in my life. She's not much of a friend, because we don't see each other outside of these classes at all, and though I have her number, I don't use it. But we walk between Enviro and Conflicts together every day, and we always sit together: her in front, me in back. I have no idea who her actual friends are, if she has many. She alludes to doing things sometimes, but she might mean doing things with her animals. Because Kate is *very* into her animals. She's on a special science track because she's going to some high-ranking veterinarian school when she graduates. It's why she's in Enviro at all. Normally she'd be in Super High-Tech Biochem III. But I think she's already taken it.

Kate is strange, but in an interesting way. She's sort of like a hipster nerd girl dreamboat in some ways, but in other ways she's just odd. Kate bites her nails—like, disgustingly bites them—and buries herself in old man cardigan sweaters that are way too big for her, even though she seems to have a decent bod, from what I can tell. Every single day she also wears these scrungy black ballet flats, and when she kicks them off under the desk in front of me, the unmistakable stink of feet wafts back. She has long, dark-brown hair with a thick fringe of bangs that hang just past her eyebrows, and she has a habit of looking up at you from under them in a way that makes you feel really small. But Kate also has plastered the inside of her locker with pictures of horses. And sheep. Really—sheep! The covers of all her notebooks are slathered with animal stickers too, and sometimes when she's done with a test or whatever, she'll put her head down and I can hear her whispering to them.

But she always pairs up with me when we have to do labs or partner projects, and she doesn't mind if she ends up doing most of the work. She writes little reminders to me during Woodham's lectures—*That thing about Kennedy is important! Make sure to reread section 5.6 at least!*—and she loves answering my swim coach's logic puzzles, which I bring her from practice. I don't know—I like her. She doesn't care what people think, and she's one of the only people I know who doesn't carry that around like some kind of medal. She's just into her own thing, period, which makes being around her sort of comforting.

Today she cares about something, though. When I walk into Enviro, she's scowling up at me from under those bangs. I can't help but feel a little better, knowing she's having a crap day too. But Chu gets class started right on time, and it isn't until our quick stroll between fifth and sixth that I get to ask her anything.

"You get your progress reports too?"

Her face is expressionless as she walks. "Sure. Why?"

"You just looked like you were maybe, I don't know—grouchy or something."

"I am grouchy. But it's not about grades. Why? Are yours bad?"

"You know mine are bad."

She blinks at me and chews on the edge of her thumbnail, spitting out little flecks of it in a way that seems she thinks I can't see.

"So why are you in a bad mood then? Me, I got plenty of excuses and"—Woodham's door is open, so we waltz in and slide into our desks—"I'm about to have another one in here."

Kate just shrugs. More scowling. More nail-biting. She shakes her head but doesn't say anything.

"Tell me or don't. I'm not going to try to guess."

She turns around and faces forward, scrunching her shoulders away from me. Whatever. She can sulk if she wants. I could really use a good distraction though, and Kate's so rarely in a bad mood that this feels significant. I'm about to tease her again, to get her to talk, but then the bell rings, and Woodham's up in front of the class, waving thin strips of paper in his giant, hairy-knuckled hand. He babbles something similar to what the rest of my teachers have said today: *Think of this as an opportunity for final improvement,* blah, blah, blah.

He moves down the first aisle, passing out each slip and offering a mumbled comment to everyone as he goes. Kate uses this as her chance to turn back around.

"Connor Bendingham."

My eyebrows go up. I actually know him. Only because he ran for class treasurer, and rumor was he cried in the guys' bathroom when he lost.

"What about him?"

"He asked me out," she hisses.

"Isn't that good?"

She glowers.

"Why isn't that good? I mean, he's decent, right?" Though I'm trying to remember exactly what he looks like. I give her a light punch on the arm, lowering my voice because Woodham's now at the top of our row. "Go you, Katie."

The thumbnail goes back in her mouth. "I don't like Connor Bendingham."

"Why not? What's wrong with him?" Except for the crybaby part, of course.

"I don't know."

"You don't know?"

But she can't answer, because Woodham's there at her desk. He hands her the slip and taps her desk twice with his finger in this way that just lets her know he's pleased.

"Miss Polonowski" is all he says, sliding my report to me. He doesn't have to say anything else. I'm barely hanging on to a D+. And if I don't pass the exam, I don't pass the class, no matter what. Which means my summer training will be screwed. I don't look at him. I don't look at Kate. I just clench my teeth, pull a deep breath in through my nose, and let it out long and slow. It's the only way to stop my heart from racing.

6

KATE DOESN'T SAY ANYTHING ELSE TO ME ABOUT THE CONNOR
Bendingham problem for the rest of the period, and I'm too
pissed about this whole day to follow up. Instead I head straight
to the pickup loop and wait for Louis: earbuds in, not looking
at anyone, blanking my mind and pretending I'm in the pool. It
works, sort of. Not as well as I want.

I avoid telling Louis about my grades, though a couple of
these reports do have to be signed—thanks, Woodham—and
then there'll be a conversation. Mom wants me to go to college because Dad didn't, and she dropped out her senior year at
Georgia State because of me. Which is fine. She can have her
dreams. It's what moms do. What she doesn't fathom, though,
is that even though we both want the same thing—she doesn't

want me to turn out like her, and I sure as shit don't want to either—that still doesn't mean I care in the same way.

Finally I'm at the pool. I ignore everyone milling around, catching up after the weekend. There are times when I can get into the rah-rah-rah togetherness and all that crap of the club, but I did enough of that at the meet on Saturday. I won for them, cheered for them. They can do without me this afternoon. I need to get into the water. I need to get my body going and let the rest take a backseat to working hard, breathing hard, just flat-out going hard.

Fortunately, Van lopes in, and we can get started. Everyone loves Van. They're all like little flowers following the path of his sunshine. Except for when he pulls shit at practice like a 200 fly while wearing athletic sneakers after we've already done probably 4,500 meters all told. Yeah. That one can suck, I won't lie. The relationship you have with your coach is definitely one of those cliché love-hate things. Even I'm not immune to it. Today he's going to go fairly easy on us though—starting with a 400 free. As I push off, the feel of the water pressing against the top of my head is a relief. As long as I let my body do what I've built and trained it to do, there's no way I can disappoint anyone else, and they can't disappoint me, either. My arm reaches up, my lungs fill when I break the surface, and then the rest of everything drops away.

• • •

After first drills, Van pulls us out for a minute to give us a pep talk, discuss the meet, and overview the afternoon's goals. This is also when he throws out the crazy logic problem-solving puzzle he's looked up on the Internet before coming to practice, in order to keep our minds sharp too. Whoever solves it first gets to pull from Van's ugly Elvis beach bag, which is full of every kind of king-size candy product known to man.

I stare at the quick notes I made while Van read the "family dinner and who sits-next-to-whom" problem aloud to us. Sounds like a freaking nightmare to me, all those people. While I'm thinking this, Grier bends over my shoulder, showing me the picture she's drawn of a craggy grandpa in giant cartoon spectacles telling his picnic tableful of smiling stick family members: *EAT ME*. I elbow her and try not to laugh.

She adds something to the drawing, cracking herself up even more, but then she suddenly stops. I look up, following her gaze to where three guys are strolling in from the locker room, Speedos barely covering their everything. Around us everyone else has stopped working on their logic too. The tallest one on the left looks a little delicate for a swimmer—like he should be an English professor or even a dancer instead. The middle guy is shorter, stockier. But then there's one on the right, so hot your eyes have to leap away: all tanned thighs and shoulders, the kind of back that makes a ski-jump curve down to his butt. His face, too, is handsome, chiseled, and full of itself.

Grier murmurs next to me, "Mama, I want my mouth on that."

And, well, duh. He is that obviously hot. But the way you can tell he knows it makes it a dumb thing to think.

Van turns and waves the guys over.

"Team, I want to introduce you to some fellows who'll be joining us for the summer—"

Grier lets out a faint squeal. I bang her with my knee to get her to shut up.

"This is Troy, Linus, and Gavin. They're going to be training with us while they're on break from their college teams. I think you'll have a lot to learn from them, but I'm sure you'll show them a thing or two, yourselves."

"Oh, I'll show him something," Grier says in a low voice, grinning devilishly.

Oh no, you won't, I immediately think. Grier really has slacked off on her training since the start of long course, so she's not going to impress anyone there. But more than that, she knows, from her experience with our teammate Dylan, how stupid it is to get involved with anyone in the club. The fallout can last for months. She's just trying to make me laugh now.

I believe this until it's time to get back into the pool, and she swishes past the new guys in this look-at-me-not-looking-at-you way. Then I'm not so sure.

• • •

It gets worse when practice is over and she grabs me by the wrist. "Come on." She's practically pulling me over toward the new guys.

I slide from her grip. "I'm not going to help you make an ass out of yourself."

"Van wants us to be nice." The last word comes out exaggeratedly from the side of her mouth. "Besides, don't you at least want to find out where they go?"

And I do. I do want to know. Because I haven't talked to anyone on a real team yet, and I need to find out what it's like. What my chances are.

"Just don't be gross."

But of course she is, right away: hand on hip, boobs out.

"So, what's up?"

"Well, hey there," the hot one says.

The pale one sticks out his hand. "Hi, I'm Troy."

We shake, officially meeting him, then Linus and Gavin, who's got beads of water rolling off his muscles like he's a waxed car.

"You got a last name, Gavin?" Grier wants to know.

"Why? You gonna Google stalk me?"

She flushes.

"Check out your times is all," I cover, though I'm not sure why. "See what you're made of."

He looks at me, curious. "Last name's Scott."

"Two last names?" Grier teases.

"Why? Who're you?"

"I'm Grier."

"I know a *guy* named Grier."

I slide my eyes away from him. That was funny.

"So, where do y'all go?" she wants to know next.

Troy and Linus have looks on their faces, the kind dork guys get when they know they've already lost out to the better-looking guy in the room, but still have to play along. UT, UF, they tell us. Gavin says, looking straight at me, "Auburn."

I try not to show I'm impressed. Auburn's not on my list, but it's mainly because their team is too good. I want to get in somewhere that needs my help, a team bad enough to give me a full ride without making me work too hard once I'm there. Still, what it took to get in there, and what it's like on the inside, would be valuable to know.

"So, what're you doing here, then?" Grier's practically batting her eyes.

Troy explains he has a job at his father's engineering company, installing electrical systems for schools. Linus is just here kicking around for the summer at his parents' place. Gavin tells us there's an internship. None of it sounds very interesting.

"Yeah, but—" Grier's toes are curling. I want to shove her. "Why us?"

"Gotta stay in shape, right?" Gavin says. And I swear, it's

like his muscles flex a little when he says it. Even Linus looks as if he wants to roll his eyes. "Besides," he goes on, "this is the only club in town with a coach who's medaled."

And it's true. I didn't care that Van had swum in the Olympics when I first joined—I just wanted someone who was going to push me so hard my brain turned to mush and my body took over. But him having those credentials helps me a lot too.

"Well, we'll see if you can keep up," I say, giving a quick we're-done-with-this smile to all of them. I tap Grier on the arm. She may want to chat all afternoon, but I've got Louis waiting for me. Besides, this is getting obvious, and therefore lame, which Grier should know, since prior to now she's the one who's taught me exactly how not to behave around guys.

"Who're you again?" Gavin says to me.

"Oh, this is Brynn," Grier answers, like I'm not worth paying attention to. Like I'm not the best swimmer on the team. Or her best friend.

"Well, nice meeting you, Brynn. Grier." Those molten chocolate eyes of his looking at both of us—interested, amused.

"Yeah, thanks." I wave. "See you tomorrow."

I figure Grier will be right on my heels, so when she's not, and still isn't in the locker room by the time I've got my clothes pulled on over my suit, I'm perplexed but also annoyed. I suck in a breath, hold it deep for a count of twenty, and then let it out slow. Oxygen always helps rejuvenate the brain. Fine.

Whatever. So she's got the hots for some new guy on the team. She'll flirt with him for a few days, and then she'll find out he's a douchebag or, worse, an actual person with feelings and opinions and problems, and then she'll get bored and drop him. I can deal with it. I've seen it before.

But on my way back out, I practically run smack into her. Her face is electric, and she's squealing.

"My phone, my phone, my phone," she gushes, scrambling to her locker and rummaging inside, murmuring numbers.

"I've gotta go, Grier. And hey—nice show out there. Way to be subtle."

But she doesn't even hear me. Instead she taps her screen and pounds her feet on the slick floor, squealing again.

"Grier, come on. Louis is—"

"Check it," she pants, coming over. "Just read it and weep."

She holds her phone up in my face. The contacts screen. HOT G it reads. That, and his number.

7

HOME. DUMP BAG. QUICK CHAT WITH MOM, AND THEN I'M OUT of the house again. It's a short walk between my place and Charlie's, but the whole time all I can think about is Grier. And Gavin. What the hell, about getting his number on the first day, acting so airheadish and dumb? What the hell about *Read it and weep?*

The place between my shoulder blades hardens beyond the usual. I mean, of course he was into her. Who wouldn't be into some pixie girl with big boobs drooling all over him? It's just that, even only a month ago, Grier had the boobs *and* she had some guts. Guys would throw themselves at her, sure, but she'd chew them up for breakfast. It was one of my very favorite things to watch. So why now? Why this guy? What the hell is happening with her—doing everything so gushy and wrong? He isn't that special. I saw his face. And, yeah, he was interested in her. Boring, obvious, fine.

Yet, if I think about it, he was also into *me*.

The idea makes me feel the sharp, intensely focused way I do right before a race. That, and a little turned on.

Charlie answers the door in a T-shirt and a pair of shorts, hair still wet from showering after his own swim practice. I'm so revved up I want to jump him right then, but first we have to small-talk with his mom and sisters before we get to go upstairs to "study." As soon as his bedroom door's shut behind him though, I grab his face and mash my mouth against his.

"Whoa, hey," he says, laughing softly while I pull off his shirt.

I kiss him again, holding onto his ribs, pulling him close, kneading the ridges of his muscles with my warm fingertips. He kisses back slower, walking us both awkwardly over to his bed. We've only actually done it twice, though we've fooled around plenty. I think, after such a long and serious relationship with Sarah, Charlie doesn't know how to just do it yet. It's like he believes it needs to be special every time.

Or that we have to talk first.

"You feeling better about earlier?" he asks, absently stroking my chest. "Grade reports?"

I shrug, thinking of Gavin, not grades. And showing Grier

what a predictable bore he is. I pull off my shirt, press my mouth hungrily against Charlie's. His hand skims down the knobby line of my backbone to cup my pointy pelvis. I press my hands flat against his shoulder blades, pulling him down with me. I want him. I want him now, now, now. No talking. No thinking.

"I really will help out," he says into my ear as I arch up under him. "We could actually, you know, study sometimes."

"Not right now though." I sigh, pushing out of my shorts and grabbing for him. His breath catches a little, and he smiles, burying his face in my neck. No, there'll be no studying—or anything else—just right now.

8

THE NEXT DAY, THANKS TO TIME WITH CHARLIE (WELL, AND the KFC Mom brought home last night), I wake up a little more refreshed, so it's easier to feel normal. I'm not any happier about grades or Grier being an asshole over Gavin, but at least I'm well rested. I'm alert in class, and I even let Charlie kiss me good-bye in the hall after lunch, though usually PDA like that gets on my nerves.

My not-great-but-not-sucky mood makes me remember Kate and that guy Connor. As soon as we're out of Enviro, I jump to the questions.

"So, what did you actually say when this guy asked you out yesterday? And remind me how you know him again?"

She scowls. "Who?"

I cock an eyebrow.

She sighs. "I told him I might already have something planned this weekend with my family. That I had to check."

"So, wait—you haven't actually said no?"

Her eyes slide in my direction; mean little slits.

"He's in my math class, okay?" she finally deadpans. "I didn't know what to tell him."

"And, so?"

"It's AP Statistics."

My brain tries to figure out why that would make it hard to know what to say when someone asks you out.

"So?"

"So, he's probably going to end up being a CPA or whiz programmer or some dork job like that. He'll probably wear golf shirts the rest of his life."

I want to tell Thrift Store Cardigan Queen that golf shirts might not be that big a problem, but I skip it. "And?"

"And, so." Looking at me like I'm dumb.

"That doesn't make sense. Why does this make him unworthy of going out with you, exactly? Okay, so, yeah, maybe one day he gets a job that pays well, where he has to wear dork outfits, but maybe that means he's doing something he likes and that he's good at?" I think of my stepdad, who wears a lot of golf shirts but is generally happy. And definitely in love with my mother. "How bad is that? Besides, there's still, you know, college in between now and your impending marriage, wherein he could turn into a real cowboy-shirt-wearer. You never know what'll happen. And college isn't until after next year. Though, wait. Are you admitting early?"

She ignores my joke and says something else from pretty much left field. "How do you know he's good at it? Stats?"

"Um, most people I know in hard-ass AP classes like that don't do it because they hate it."

"I do," she says quiet. "I hate statistics."

I'm high with myself. I might actually be able to help her. Because I know all about getting through things you hate. "Is that why you don't like him?"

If she says yes, I will explain that conquering something you hate is an excellent motivator. An absolutely fantastic thing to make you stronger.

Her mouth twists down. "It's not like that."

We're standing outside the classroom now.

"Well, is he ugly?"

"No."

"Does he stink?"

"I don't think so. He sits two rows away."

"Did he stink when he asked you out?"

She thinks about it. "No."

"Does he have some kind of donkey laugh or something?"

She giggles. "No."

"Excessively hairy knuckles?"

"Okay, cut it out. I get your point."

"Eczema?"

She's really laughing now. "He might. He wears a lot of long-sleeve T-shirts."

"Okay, so it's either eczema or a dangerous affection for Dave Matthews Band and hacky sacks."

"Or surfing." She points to the Ron Jon logo on my own long-sleeve tee.

I hold up my finger. "No, surfing isn't bad. I'm not sure where they'd do it around here, but those surfers are mad skilled." I wink.

She blushes. Which makes me even more determined to get her to say yes to this guy. To get excited about something other than border collies for once in her life. I can teach this girl. I know all the right tricks.

"C'mon. Have you ever really talked to him?" I ask.

Shrug. "Not really. A little in a group project. Sometimes before class."

"So how do you know how awful he is? You're a smart girl. And this is stupid. Just say yes to the poor guy, ball breaker."

She smiles up from under those bangs. "I don't know."

I give her a playful shove into the room as the bell rings and Woodham heads up to the board. "Well, it's all over your face that you want to, dummy. And if you don't say yes to him, I'm going write him a note and do it for you."

"Ugh . . . no, don't," she growls.

I smile.

"Fine," she says.

I win.

9

AFTER CLASS I'M SO JAZZED ABOUT MY LITTLE VICTORY WITH Kate that I actually tell Louis about it in the car on the way to practice, surprising us both with my teenage daughterliness. Reminding Kate about getting through things you hate also makes me confident that I can totally put up with Grier's twitterpation for another day or week, or however short it lasts, because ultimately that's all it will be. And if I have to bounce her on the ass to speed up the process, so be it. We both know I'm stronger, and I can do anything.

Even when Shyrah comes up behind me saying, "New guys, huh?" in this cowed way, I just laugh.

"What about them?"

"I dunno." He looks uneasily at some of the other girls.

"Don't worry about it, Shy. You're still our prince. Old guys like them hanging around just makes you look more studly."

"You think they're any good?" Dylan says, coming over. Megan and Siena are also half-watching, pretending not to listen.

"Haven't seen enough of them to know. But could be a good challenge."

"I just don't want extra dudes in my lane," Siena grumbles, joining us for real.

Megan nods.

"So, tell Van you're on your period."

Siena makes a face and moves off the bleachers. Whatever. Gavin and his friends are nothing to worry about.

"Look," I say, "these are full-of-themselves college douchebags. They're not gunning for the same things you are anymore. You guys can totally smoke them. And if you can't, then I will."

"True that." Dylan nods, giving me a high five. I don't know for sure if Gavin and his friends are actually lazy, but it sure sounds good. And I will smoke them.

"So, come on, guys." I jostle Shyrah on the shoulder. "Stop pouting like a bunch of pussies and get ready to show."

Two seconds later Grier rushes in, hooking her arm over my shoulder.

"Did you get my message?" She's so close, I can feel her fluttering eyelashes on my cheek.

"What message?"

She squeals like an excited little pig. "Check it."

She punches up the message she's apparently sent me and then waves it in my face. Because she's laughing, her hand's moving around too much for me to see anything, so I grab her wrist to hold the phone still. At first I can't tell what it is, because the image is blurred and there isn't a lot of light. But then Grier giggles again, and I realize it's Gavin's face, nestled between her boobs.

The cocky, bubbly feeling I had just a minute ago crashes to my stomach. I push her phone down so she doesn't see how bothered I am.

"When the hell did that happen?" *And why are you humping him so fast? And taking pictures? And seriously, what the hell?*

"Last night." Grier tells me quiet, eyes glinting.

Last night? "How?"

"I texted him," she rushes, putting her phone away because Megan's headed over with that nosy expression on her face. "I got bored, wasn't doing anything. He came over."

There are about sixty things to say trapped behind my tongue, including how trashy and desperate that makes her look, but before I can decide which one to deliver first, Megan reaches us and goes, "Who came over?"

Megan is one of those unfortunate Hulk girls you often see in swimming. She can't really help it, but the way she compensates for her bigness by trying to be the most popular girl on the team is even more unfortunate than her size.

"Oh, no one," Grier trills, looking pointedly at Gavin, who's just walked in from the locker room.

Megan hits Grier on the arm. "Shut up." But her face is delighted.

"Well, I couldn't wait around letting him figure out how hot you are, could I?"

She's talking to Megan. I know she's talking to Megan. But it's as though, for a second, she's also talking to me. I'm speechless, but Grier doesn't even notice. She just gives us both a little wave and skips over to Gavin, who's watching her with sex-drunk eyes.

"She is such a bitch," Megan mutters.

I make my voice light, like I couldn't care less. "Nah, just bored. Besides, you know how Grier is with guys."

"Yeah, I do," Megan huffs. "And it's getting pretty boring."

"Well, you probably won't have to suffer long."

"Sure. It's not like we have another whole year with her or anything."

"Oh, I don't know," I say, narrowing my gaze. "Something might make her burn out long before that."

• • •

Swim.

Push.

Breathe.

Swim.

Swim and swim, and that is all.

At one point during practice, while we're at the end of our lanes waiting for the next set of instructions from Van, Gavin looks across the ropes and waves at me. I give him a tight, dismissive smile. I don't know what to think about him, or her, so I duck my head under the water and push off, so I won't have to.

10

"SO, I GUESS I OWE YOU ONE," KATE SAYS TO ME THE NEXT day in Enviro. She has this serious, almost morbid look on her face, and I can tell she's being sarcastic. I haven't been in much of a good mood myself today—Charlie wanted to be all grab-handy and gooey-gooey at lunch, which I guess is my fault because of Monday afternoon, plus another help-me-forget-about-Grier session yesterday after we both finished practice. I feel bad, a little, for being so crabby. I don't know.

But then I realize Kate's smiling.

It makes me smile too. "You didn't!"

She nods. "Yesterday. Your pep talk. I thought about it, and I realized you were right. So just a minute ago in Stats I went over to him before class and I said, 'If you're still up for something Friday, turns out I'm free.'"

"'Turns out you're free'? So formal of you."

"I don't know what we're doing or how I even really feel about it, but it's better not to think too much, right?" She looks so pretty. Confident. "So I owe you one."

"Unless of course he's a suck kisser."

She turns scarlet. "Well—"

"Good for you, Kate." And I mean it.

"I guess you just give good advice is all."

She smiles again and then turns around to get out her homework for today, leaving me to think about that. I do give good advice. Because I know what I'm talking about. So maybe it's time for me to follow some of it myself instead of doing all this sulking.

At the beginning of practice, before Grier can show me another effed-up photo, I suggest we all go out for burritos after. Grier can play whatever whorish games with Gavin she wants. I'm just not going to let her make me look like a loser while she does.

As soon as I tell her my idea, her eyes go over to Louis, hunched on the bleachers, waiting. "What about—?"

I shrug. "Forget him. I'll just tell him we have girl stuff. At this point he'd probably come watch practice even if I wasn't on the team anymore."

She laughs, but I can see she still wants Gavin to herself.

"C'mon," I say, nudging her. "We'll ask the other guys too if you want. I need to get to know your new boyfriend a little anyway, right?"

Her face lights up. "Oh man, you wouldn't believe—"

But I don't want to hear it. I stop her by moving over to Gavin, who's been lingering around, watching us both.

"Some workout, right?" I say brightly. "I thought we could all go for some burritos or something after practice. I'm starved. And I want to hear more about Auburn."

I drape my arm around Grier's neck, showing him how buddy-buddy we are.

"Sound's cool," he says, leering at Grier.

Grier tries to match my chipperness, now that Gavin's into it. "Sure!"

"Cool then." Behind Grier's back I twirl my fingers at Gavin.

When practice is over, Louis offers to drive us, but I tell him Grier can just give me a lift home, even though our house is about the most opposite direction from hers. After he's gone, I explain to her that he's got some work he had to bring home and can't wait around for me or give me a ride. The expression of annoyance on her face makes me feel a small stab of rage toward her for obviously wanting to ditch me so fucking quickly, but I take a deep breath and blow it out slow.

As soon as we've slid into the booth—Gavin and Grier on one side, me across from them—I say to Gavin right off: "So, is it hard?"

Grier briefly glares at me. Gavin looks surprised.

I keep my face innocent. "At Auburn, I mean."

The corners of his mouth lift. "Sure, it's, um, hard." There's a crinkling around his eyes. "Probably not anything you can't handle though."

I level my eyes at him, breathe through my nose.

"What about long? I mean, in a really exhausting kind of way? The kind where you just feel like you can't walk or do anything afterward? Or instead do they, you know, go easy on you sometimes? Take things slower?"

He swallows before he answers, but his eyes are sparking. "I guess it's just like your own experiences. Drive really hard then pull back, rest a bit. So that you're ready for the final push."

Grier's looking back and forth at us, not sure whether we're joking or not.

"And what about tryouts?" I go on. "Was it hard to, you know, get in?"

This time he smiles full on. Cocky, no-of-course-it's-not-hard-to-get-in smile.

"For some, yeah. I think I had the scouts impressed pretty quick though."

"Good times, then?"

"Pardon?"

"Your times." Like I'm talking to a deaf grandpa. "Are they any good?"

His eyebrow arches. "Probably not as good as yours."

From under the table, I feel his foot very purposefully connect with mine.

"Brynn is the fastest fly in the whole state," Grier chimes in then, like I'm her kid. Or more now like suddenly I'm valuable to her again, since Gavin's clearly enjoying this. "She's the fastest Van's had in his club for years. She could go Olympic."

"That has yet to be determined," I grumble.

"Pretty much from the meets, though," she says.

"And at State you go for National time too, right?" Gavin says.

I shrug. "Sure."

The energy around the whole table has shifted. I don't like trying to have normal talk with this guy.

"That'll score you some," he says, grinning, like he's read my mind.

I grin back, feeling crazy and powerful. "Yeah, I'd like to be able to see myself looking at five, maybe six at once."

This time his eyebrows frown down together.

"Um, I don't think you want that many scouts on you, really. One, maybe two solid interests will be able to give you what you want." His voice has slowed down, changed pitch. He doesn't want to play anymore, which I guess is fine, since our food arrives and I'm dying to eat. We all know who just won that round, anyway.

• • •

g thks ur cool Grier texts me later, after she's dropped me off.

thx

he wts us 2 go 2 sm party this wknd

I wait. *Us* could mean just her and him, after all. She could just be rubbing this in my face.

r u dng anythg? comes in a minute later.

I smile.

going 2 a party i guess. ☺

||

FRIDAY MORNING, ALONG WITH REGULAR SWIM STUFF, I PACK party clothes and an extra suit in my gear bag. Gavin didn't say where exactly this party was—some friend of a friend of his— but he did emphasize that it would likely be wild. So I made sure to seem intrigued, plus bring a little insurance so I don't miss practice in the morning.

At lunch, when Charlie asks about my plans, I shrug and say the same thing I usually do: "Grier's, practice, homework, cemetery." This time it's harder to sound like I'm not lying, though. We tried to do a couple of date-ish things when we got back from the UGA meet and wanted to keep hanging out, but both times I got this impatient, itchy feeling that I couldn't shake. Charlie being a swimmer too means I don't have to explain my life to him, except when he wants to know about my non-swimming life. I like it better when I'm at his place and can just get up and go after we make out, instead of having to sit there with all his get-to-know-each-other questions. Not that it isn't nice that he wants to. I don't know. We should try again, I guess. We will. But tonight I have other plans that definitely can't involve him.

"What about you?" I ask, trying to sound apologetic and encouraging.

"Eh. Guys getting together at Ethan's, I think. I might go for a while."

I nod. Like most of us, Charlie's not up much for the late-night social crowd either. Plus, he actually works at his grades.

"But maybe we can study Sunday?" he asks, grinning.

I smile back. "Oh, I think we could probably work some of that in."

It's Kate I really want to talk to about the weekend. Connor's taking her to some coffeehouse with live music for their date tonight. She told me all about it yesterday. I think it sounds kind of lame, but he's obviously making an effort, so points to him in the long run. And Kate was almost giggly cute about it. The transformation from Monday was remarkable.

Today, though, she's a wreck.

"Get your fingers out of your mouth." I pull her spittle-slick thumb down to the desk. "You can't be doing that all night with him."

"I can't help it. I don't even know I do it."

"You can help it, and you do know. Look, whenever you find your teeth crunching down on fingernail—hell, when you find your hand going up to your mouth—just recognize it and force yourself to do something else. Like, jam it down between your thighs maybe—"

She grimaces.

"Okay, or just lightly scratch the inside of your other arm. Not enough to make marks—just a tickle."

"You're serious."

I almost grab her. "You can make yourself do anything if you put your mind to it. All that shit they say is really true. The trick, though, is *really* putting your mind to it."

"So, what can I put my mind to so I can keep my stomach from being full of rocks, then? Or to keep my parents from asking embarrassing questions? I really think I should cancel. I don't think I feel well. Maybe it was my lunch—"

Her hand starts going back up to her mouth. I clear my throat pointedly, and she drops it back down, giving her other arm a halfhearted tickle. That jacked-up feeling I had getting her to say yes to this date comes over me again.

"You're just nervous. It's okay. Nervousness is mostly your

body's way of getting ready for something new. It's not a bad thing. But you don't have to be ruled by it."

I have to stop because the bell's rung, and Chu's picking up the questions on last night's reading. I give her what I managed to conquer (three out of five isn't bad), and take out another piece of paper.

You just have to recognize what's going on and decide to be the master, I write to Kate. *You're more than just your feelings. You can recognize what's going on and change your own reaction to them. You can even change the reactions of other people. It's completely empowering.*

I believe this—I know this—so firmly, it's like I'm carving the words into the paper. I pass the note over to her. It takes her a minute to respond.

Yeah, but when the horses are nervous about something, they're usually right, she responds.

I snort. I guess I shouldn't be surprised she'd say something like that. I write back.

Horses are different. Are you a horse? No, you are not. Neither are you a pig, donkey, sheep, dog, kitten, or goldfish. Horses get nervous because they don't understand that if they focus, they can actually kick the shit out of any person or coyote or whatever is coming around. They don't remember how fast they are, how high they can jump. Dogs forget that they can pretty much kill anything they want to, even their own masters. Sheep—well, there's no argument there. Sheep are fucking stupid. But you're not a sheep. You're not trapped, and you're not a follower. You're doing this because you want to, because it's different and exciting. If it sucks, you don't have to do it again. That's the thing. Unlike sheep, you can actually learn from your experiences. But you're not going to if you don't have some of them.

She doesn't write me back for the rest of class, which is irritating, but also it means she knows I'm right. I'm so pleased, I even register most of the lecture and raise my hand when Chu asks for questions.

On the way to last period though, Kate's on me right away.

"Okay, I'm not going to get into a debate with you on the differences between humans and animals, because you're just—" She holds a flat palm out and makes a crazy circle. "Okay?"

"Um. Okay."

She takes a deep breath. "It's not the same for you, and you don't understand. You can't manipulate people like that. Or emotions. But you do have a point about experiences, and that's why I'm even halfway listening to you. I thought in class about how the only way to train an animal to do new things is to repeat behavior over and over with them, and so that is the only reason I'm not canceling on Connor right now. Because the way to learn new things is to go through the motions of them. So, I'll try it. But don't go thinking you're so smart. Because there *are* similarities, and there are reasons why animal instinct can be superior sometimes. Still, I'm going. I said I'm going, and I'm going."

She's so intense, it's hard not to laugh at her. But I don't, because she's still doing this even though she's scared, and I'm proud. I'd almost hug her if we were good enough friends to do that.

"I'm glad you came to that conclusion," I say instead. "Glad that I could help."

"You're not a help. You just conveniently reminded me of something I already knew." She jerks open the door to Woodham's class and holds it for me. "If you want to help me, you'll tell me what you think I should wear."

I don't know much about Kate's wardrobe, so most of my suggestions are dumb ones like "Pocahontas costume" or "A dress made of tires," but it's fun coming up with ways to make her laugh, and in some ways it reminds me of my middle-school pals. At the bottom of my note—which I hand her at the end of class—I remind her that the guy asked her out with her looking the way she does at school. So there's no way she can lose.

12

AS SOON AS I CROSS INTO THE NEARLY PALPABLE WALL OF chlorine that surrounds the pool, it surprises me that the day was so good, I wasn't already dying to get here. At the same time, I can also feel my body sharpen up, focusing. Good meet or not last weekend, there are still two hundredths to shave off my time before State. I waggle my neck back and forth, bounce up and down on my toes twenty times, and then twist my trunk until I'm almost dizzy. It clears my head of Kate. Of my teammates wandering in and saying hey. Of Gavin, waving a hello at me but keeping his distance. Even of Grier, who pads across the water-slick floor, smiling, obviously ready to show me something else sick on her phone. I wave at them both but keep working the rubber of my swim cap down around the back of my head and pressing my goggles to my face. Breathe. This is what you're here for. Just this and nothing else.

This is how it goes: 200 free. Warming up. Then four 200s on skips: freestyle, kickboard, pull buoy, then free. Out for pep talk and logic problems. Then we split up into sprinters and long-distance swimmers. Today it's four 500 IMs for us in long distance: 125 fly, 125 backstroke, 125 breast, 125 free, all within a certain time. I barely see my teammates at this point in practice, just the water and my hands and the blank space that is me, breathing and moving and pushing forward. We catch our breaths at the end of the pool for a moment while Van directs the college guys. I hear Siena and Sam talk about their weekends—mostly studying by the sounds of it—some science project—and then it's under the water again for more.

An hour after being back in the water, we're at the peak of practice, which is when you can begin to tire out, especially since you know that whatever comes after this set is just going to be worse. This is when you can begin to think that Van just sits in his cushy office all morning dreaming up the most complicated ways in which he can torture you, break you down, and drive you to tears. It's when you can start thinking about all the other kids in your grade, lying around in front of video games or strolling together at Atlantic Station, maybe skateboarding a bit or, at worst, chasing after a soccer or football. It's when you can begin to wonder what the hell you're doing, driving your body like this in a pursuit that will not crown you Most Popular or even Most Athletic, because all anyone cares about is soccer, football, and cheerleading. It's the part of the day where your chest is starting to heave and you've stopped feeling the difference between water and air, because you're not in the air long enough to remember how it feels before you're back in the water again.

But it's also the best part. Because if you can blank your mind and zone past the groaning of everyone else—the beating of your own heart, and the amused smile on Van's face—your body can push you to a place your mind was too stupid and too lazy to believe in. You just have to do it and swim. You have to know you can and then leave the rest at the edge of the pool.

Last set is for time. When I get out, Van shows me: 1:05, 1:04, 1:05, and then 1:02. He rubs the top of my cap. "Exceptional," he says. "Keep this up, and there are no worries about State."

"Thanks, Van." My voice is breathy. My whole self is breathy. In. Out. In. Out. In. Out. It won't stop coming, but I know it's okay because it's just what my lungs have to do to fuel the muscles. I shake my shoulders, wrists, ankles. It's something to do while everyone else clambers out, looks at their own times, has a word or so with Van, and begins to get their things. In. Out. In. Out. Starting to slow a little bit as I picture a roller coaster coming to a stop. Because it is just like that: You were in, it was crazy, and now it's over. You're not even sure you can remember what happened. You're not sure you care.

. . .

On my way to the locker room with Grier, I see Gavin watching me, even while he's talking to Linus and Troy. Not Grier, but me. He's trying to pretend like he isn't, but he is. I catch him at it just the once. And then I know I don't need to look at him again until later tonight.

13

IT TAKES THREE INTRODUCTIONS FOR ME TO UNDERSTAND that the girl hosting this party's name is Fancy.

Not a nickname. Not a middle name. But her honest-to-god, given-while-the-umbilical-is-being-cut name. It sends snorts of laughter out my nose that I can't stop. Part of the problem is the pre-party party Grier and I had at her house after practice, getting ready. She was wild and psyched about Gavin, saying all this crazy shit about how he's her future: garbage she would've died to hear herself say even six weeks ago. In part to get her to shut up, and in part to keep myself from caring, we did shots of this amazing cinnamon stuff called Fireball that makes your mouth feel like the inside of a dragon's. After a while we danced around her giant bedroom then made each other up. Even in spite of the Gavin crap, it was fun like we haven't had in maybe months.

Since I won't stop laughing about the Fancy thing, Grier pulls me into the kitchen. It's full of people, and there are sticky pools of soda, liquor, and who knows what on the huge granite island already, though it's not even nine o'clock. The cabinets are big enough to get inside of, and I whisper to Grier that we should play hide-and-seek. She only half-smiles, cool. I realize she's looking for Gavin, and the silliness in me washes away. I predict she'll stick with me until we find him, but that's it.

As the happy feeling dissolves, I straighten my face and move ahead of her to weave through the kitchen. If that's how it is now, fine. We meet some girls. We meet some guys. I try to get into conversations with as many people as I can. Because of this I find out that the little sister of our lovely hostess Fancy is named Nimby, and I nearly spit my drink out. Which is fine, because I know I'm more than a little drunk. For me it doesn't take very much, and it's already been a lot. After a while Grier's arm loosens from mine. Gavin must be here. I'm not going to follow her—I'm not going to care—so I grab some water and go to dance around the sunken living room with a bunch of people I don't know. Five songs? Six? I'm unsure of the time, only that Grier's ditched me, so I have to wait around long enough to make it look like it was my idea.

Finally, after I think I've danced at least a little of the booze off, I head outside for some air. I stumble down a series of stone steps that remind me of a garden in a book, and then I'm standing on this huge stone patio around a Jacuzzi with an actual waterfall going into it. Grier, Gavin, and that guy Linus and two other girls are there. They look up at me. Especially Gavin—glad but pretending not to be. Grier fake-squeals and asks me where I've been.

"Dancing," I say, like she cared at all.

I sit down on the cement, a foot or two away from the edge of the Jacuzzi. Everyone seems to have their suits intact, though Linus's clothes are piled behind him. There's a pair of boxer briefs right on top, but he's sitting there as if he's in a living room recliner. I decide I like Linus. Not *like* him, like him, but like him. He's a good guy. He doesn't deserve to be just Gavin's sidekick. Maybe I'll set him up with Siena. Or Kelly.

Then Gavin says, "So you, sport," to me, like no one else is there. The steam between us makes it seem like he's sitting in a giant bowl of soup. His lips are also very red. "Pretty impressive, eh?"

I sit up straighter, blink a few times. "What's impressive?"

"Your times, man."

I laugh. "Man." Is he really going to talk about my times? Here? In front of Grier and everyone else?

"Fly's your thing, right?"

I nod. "Fly's my thing."

"What's your two hundred?"

I laugh again, low, trying to take in my breath. I did kick ass in practice today. And I know he noticed.

"Right now? Two-eleven-six."

He whistles. I shrug. It isn't a horrible time. But it is ten seconds behind the world record for long course. Still, I watch Grier see Gavin being impressed with me. I lean back farther on my hands and open my knees a little.

"So, the scouts are on you already, huh?" he asks, eyes glinting like they were the other night when we went to get burritos.

Everybody else is bored though, talking about something else. I'm bored too—that dirty flirt talk game's already been done.

"I've heard not till summer."

He shakes his head. "This is when they should start looking at you. Olympic trials will be here before you know it."

"Not for me." I shake my head, enjoying the floppy feel of it.

"You serious?"

"Sure I'm serious. You're not serious about them, are you?"

He laughs. From what I've been able to tell, Gavin's a decent swimmer. Good enough to get into Auburn and stay there, anyway. But I know he's not serious because of the internship. You don't take summer jobs if you're gunning for the gold. You don't have time to. Sometimes you don't even go to college.

"Well," he finally says, in that dismissive-dad-sounding way. "I just mean—"

"You ever swim against Kenyon, Wake, or Brown?"

This part I want to know. I want to know how far I could

maybe reach. Those schools are probably still too academic to be of much interest—it's not like I want to study my ass off for a degree that'll get me basically nothing, either—but they're far away, and I'm curious.

Grier's had enough though, apparently. She gets up, reaching for Gavin's wrist.

"There's karaoke in there somewhere," she says. "This is supposed to be fun."

Everyone else stands, finds their towels and shirts. Linus shows up beside me all of a sudden, somehow clothed. I hook my arm with his, grabbing one of the girls with my other elbow, making buddy-buddy.

"So who's got a favorite song?" I lilt, trying to make myself sound happy and carefree, instead of—again—as though I'm being poked hard in the ass by the reject stick.

In response Linus quotes some rap I've never heard before, and I laugh loud. Before I turn up the stone steps, I see Grier pouting by the edge of the Jacuzzi. Gavin puts his arms loosely around her waist and murmurs something near her mouth. She swings away from him wildly, but he swoops her down in a stupid dip. He bites his lower lip. She's laughing now and bumps her pelvis against his. They're probably not coming up for karaoke. Which is fine—I will. I'll party. I'll mingle. I'll have a good time. But first I make sure Gavin sees me looking back at him before I disappear with everyone else up the stairs.

14

ELEVEN O'CLOCK? TWELVE? GAVIN AND GRIER HAVE BEEN GONE
a long time. I've had some kind of melon stuff, and I'm sure fourteen people have sung Adele at least twice. My butt's numb. I
need to pee. And maybe get some water and find somewhere to
lie down, since it's obvious we're not heading home anytime soon.

I climb the stairs and head down the hall, sliding my hand
along the creamy wallpaper, moving toward what I think is a
bathroom. It's late. I need to wash my face, get to sleep. There's
practice tomorrow, and I still need to work hard. I'm halfway
down the hall when someone comes up behind me and grabs
my waist.

"You're so hot." He breathes in my ear, scratching me with
his dark stubble.

Without thinking, I reach up, grab the back of his head, and press my butt against him. When his hand goes up inside my shirt, sliding steadily up over my ribs, I finally realize what I'm doing and turn around.

"You leave my friend passed out by the Jacuzzi?"

His hands move down, hot on my hips, moving in small circles. I'm shocked, but I don't try to pull away.

"She's fine. Talking to some guy about Bali."

"Yeah, she likes doing that."

He leans even closer. "She likes talking about you, is what."

We're both drunk. This is crazy and stupid, and—

"Oh, yeah? And what do you like talking about?"

"I think you have an idea."

There's a flare of heat in my crotch. "What, yourself? How awesome it is at Auburn?"

His hand presses harder. "Why do you have to be such a bitch to me?"

I smile. I can't help it. It's something I do at an intimidating meet, too.

"You're going to have to do more than maul me in the hall-way at some party while I'm on the way to take a piss if you want me to be nicer. Maybe also stop flirting with me while you're screwing my friend. And oohing and aahing over my times, too. Like nobody else ever does that."

"Oh, I'll ooh and ah," he growls, guiding me against the

wall and lowering his mouth toward mine, completely ignoring my comment about Grier or the idea of Grier altogether. All I see is the redness of his lips again. The glinting ivory of his teeth. All I feel is the racing of my heart. I both want him to kiss me and don't.

There's a noise on the stairs. "Whoa, dude, sorry."

A guy in a hoodie with the sleeves cut off stumbles toward us. "This the bathroom?" He points, boozy, down the hall.

The warmth of embarrassment, and maybe relief, rushes over me. I wiggle away from Gavin.

"Do you mind if I use it first?"

Without waiting for an answer, I hurry down the hall and yank open the door at the end, which is, fortunately, a cavernous bathroom. Full of orchids. I lock the door behind me without looking back and turn on the water, hard. I lean over the sink, arms locked and straight to keep them from shaking. I take in deep breaths—one . . . two . . . three . . . four—blowing them out equally slow. Finally I pull my head up straight to look in the mirror. My eyes are bleary, and my face is flushed.

But after a few seconds of blinking back fear, my mouth starts to twist, and soon I'm grinning.

15

MORNING.

Early—maybe six o'clock by the light coming through the window?

I'm curled in a fetal position in the middle of a bathtub that might be as big as my bed. I'm not sure how I ended up here—though I do remember a vague need to get to the bathroom. I climb out, head raging. But my body knows what to do: pee first. I prop myself up with my forearms on my knees, head hanging down. It is so heavy. Fireball, I guess, and then that green melon shit and then I don't even know what. I don't remember details, though I do remember screaming "Me and Bobby McGee" into the karaoke mic. Did I get up there and do a duet with someone? Ugh. I think I did. And then there was Gavin in the hall.

A clock on the elaborate sink across from me says 6:18. I pat myself on the shoulder. Even hung over I know when to wake myself up. On Saturdays practice isn't until eight, so I could conceivably find an actual bed or couch and get a little more sleep right now. But I don't know exactly what or who I'd stumble on if I did that, and it's better to stay upright and keep moving.

Mainly I need aspirin. And some water. I've also got to get out of here. I peel myself up off the john and lean into the mirror over the sink. My eyes are bloodshot with puffy little bags underneath them. I pull down the lower lids with my fingertips and then give myself a couple of wake-up pats on both cheeks. I look like ass. I feel like ass. Van is totally going to know that I was partying. He'll give me some kind of annoying talk. Whatever. I'll still do fine. And if not, I'll make the team all feel a little better about themselves, not douching them for once. Either way, I win.

I straighten up, pull my shoulders back, and take a deep breath. Hold it. Hold it some more. My lung capacity is twice as much as most people's. I could hold my breath for twenty minutes if my stupid brain didn't need the oxygen. If there weren't the whole involuntary passing-out element, I could probably hold my breath my whole life.

I let the breath out. Wash my face with the expensive exfoliating wonder cream I find in the shower. I press my face into the deep plush towel and leave a ghost impression in it. I consider getting into that Jacuzzi outside, but I know I'm also probably dehydrated, and the heat might not be such a good thing. I bounce up and down on my toes, pat my cheeks again, this time a little harder. I open the medicine cabinet, but there's nothing in there besides a snap-on head for a Sonicare and two tampons in their pearly pink paper. I take one more look at myself in the mirror, at all those freckles, those tired eyes.

"You will master this," I say to the girl in the mirror.

Downstairs in the sticky, muddy kitchen, I gulp down so much water, my stomach hurts until I make myself burp. I find some aspirin and take three of them just to be sure. My head's still heavy, but moving around feels better. I twirl my arms in their sockets—one, two, one, two—and shrug a few times, loosening. I fight the desire to lie back down. It would be better to get to the pool early, swim out part of this hangover. Though I should try to find something to eat.

I end up leaving Grier a note in her purse—conveniently piled in the first bedroom downstairs with some jackets and one discarded umbrella—and take her keys. It occurs to me that she had no intention of going to practice this morning, which pisses me off. Sure, we've goofed around before, stayed up late, and even partied, but we always knew there was practice. Even if we stayed up all night, she'd be there with me at the pool the next morning. It's part of why we made such a good pair.

In her car I punch in the address of the pool and let Grier's GPS take me there. At least I intuited enough to toss my gear bag in the back before we left her house. I'll stop and get some grapefruit juice and an egg sandwich on the way, maybe even shower in the locker room. By the time everyone arrives, Van will never know. I'll show them both.

As soon as he comes in, Van stands at the edge of the pool and just watches me in the water. I'm sluggish and unimpressive, but at least I'm swimming. He doesn't say anything, even when practice starts.

Dolphin for fifty, then backstroke for fifty, and then dolphin for fifty again.

Breathing patterns.

Out for talk and logic. Today I don't try to get the problem right, even though one of those king-size PayDays would be pretty freaking good right now. Van doesn't ask me where Grier is, but Megan does, making it clear she has a pretty solid idea where, since Gavin isn't here either. Fucking stupid—both of them skipping practice on the same day. Why don't you take out an advertisement, guys? Even Linus made it—he gave me a sympathetic little smile when he came in.

At one point Van gives me a look. I feel myself wanting to

pull my eyes away from him, but I don't. I stick it out, hold his gaze. He's the one who looks away.

Three 500s, kickboard, speeding up each time.

Four 100 IMs, descending time.

Two 150s, each on 3:20. Then two more, each on 2:15. Fifty after that, easy.

Two hundred fly, fast as I can go, which, unfortunately, isn't that fast once I look at the clock. It's not like I'm thinking—I'm not thinking—but I'm more aware of the water this morning. It keeps splashing up at me, getting in my face. I'm trying to scoop it up with my arms, but today it's so heavy.

16

WHEN I GET BACK TO MY BAG AND MY PHONE, GRIER'S TEXTED me about twenty times, first wondering where I am and then getting mad and then finding my note and figuring it out and saying to come back and pick her up after practice because Gavin's got something to do. I want to type back about how convenient it is, her worrying about me once she needs me, but whatever. This way we'll go back to her place and eat something. I can hear what happened with them after the whole Hallway Hey There. If Gavin said anything about me.

"What happened to you?" Grier wants to know when she gets in the car. There are mascara smears around her eyes. If she had any hair, it'd be sticking up on end.

"Um, practice?"

"No, I mean last night."

"I went and did karaoke like we said. A few people were actually good. This one dude did a dead-on Usher." I'm making this up. Or I might kind of remember. I don't know. I press my head against the headrest on the seat. Suddenly my arms feel like they might sink into the leather.

"Oh. Gavin said he saw you and you weren't feeling that great. I didn't know where you went."

Well, that's at least interesting.

"I was okay. I was singing. What about you? I thought you were coming up."

"Oh, we hung out."

More of that stupid glimmer in her eyes.

"Well, I hope you had fun."

"Good God. His mouth is so—"

I don't want to hear it. "I had fun too."

And it's enough to stop her. At least get her to change direction. "I'm so glad. Because he wants us to go out again tonight."

I consider that. "I don't know. I'm pretty tired."

Until this week, that'd be enough to let her know that what I really want is just a standard sleepover at her place: her and me and some videos, maybe a crazy stunt, a decadent pig-out. It'd be enough to tell her that I hate people, and I've had enough of them for now, including Gavin.

Instead, out of the corners of my eyes, I see her clutch the steering wheel harder.

"Why don't you just come out and say you don't like him?"

Even though I'm expecting some kind of response, this one's a surprise.

"What?"

"You think I can't tell by that mocking look you get on your face whenever he's around, the way you're always making fun of him, pretending you think he's cool?"

She's definitely been preparing this speech.

"I don't even know him. You don't either, for that matter."

"He thinks you're awesome, you know," she says. "He thinks you could really be something, even if he barely knows you."

Ha. That's funny. I close my eyes.

"Seems like he's a game-player is all," I finally say.

"So?"

It takes all my strength not to tell her she'll lose if she plays this way.

"If that's what you're into, fine," I say instead. "Used to be you were the player though."

She pauses, stunned. I am a little too.

"How do you know I'm still not?"

My eyes stay closed, so I can't see her, but I can tell from her voice that she's got that prissy look on her face again.

"That stuff you said about him being the future last night, for one thing. But it's more than that. The way you are around the pool. Showing off."

"We do not show off."

I finally look at her. "Maybe you're not. But the whole team knows what you're doing." I picture Megan's jealous face.

She doesn't have a response. She knows the scope of what I mean, but all she can say is, "Well."

I don't sigh out loud, but my whole body feels it. "Whatever." I toss my head. "It only makes practice worse for you, because Van's obviously pissed about it. But maybe that's part of your game. Just don't—"

It registers to me that we're almost back at my house.

"Wait. We're not hanging at your place?"

Guilt seizes her face. "Later Gavin and I are—"

I don't give her the satisfaction of finishing that sentence. "Fine."

"But I'll pick you up later, and we'll go to that party, right? It should be way more chill. Not so many sorority girls. It's at some lake. Really, it'll be cool."

"Whatever. I just need to sleep, anyway."

"Brynn, it's not like that. I'm not going to be one of those girls, I swear. We're still hanging out tonight. You're coming, right? I think Gavin really wants you to."

Ha.

"Whatever," I concede. I'm tired. I need to get out of this car. "Text me later about it, I guess."

As I climb out and grab my gear, it crosses my mind that not sleeping in a bathtub and not getting up at six a.m. for a two-and-a-half-hour practice must mean you're fresh and ready for an afternoon fuckfest. I suppose our usual tradition of going to lunch (thanks, Mr. and Mrs. Hawkins's infinite credit limit) and then crashing awhile before hanging out again isn't enough of a happening for her anymore. I guess Gavin's wang is all the dare she needs to swallow to make her feel fulfilled. So, fine. I'll go back home and crawl into my own bed.

Later tonight I'll be the one who's refreshed.

17

MOM AND LOUIS ARE BOTH SURPRISED WHEN GRIER PULLS into the driveway. They're outside doing yard work, both of them in work gloves, baggy T-shirts, and shorts—clothing neither of them really should be wearing anywhere, but especially not outside where anyone can see them. I jump out and Grier waves, pulling back out before they make it over to her car.

"Everything okay?" Mom wants to know.

"How was practice?" Louis asks.

I can tell they're pretending to be cheerful about my unexpected presence on their little Saturday together. Avoiding this time with them is a large part of my usual weekend stay-overs at Grier's. I'm not interested in perusing junky flea markets or apple-picking or even going to see a movie with them more times than necessary.

"Grier's mom's in town but just for the weekend," I lie. "They had to do some stuff."

"Oh. Well, are you hungry?" Louis asks. "And if you're up for bagging some of these leaves, we would certainly welcome the help." The giant magnolia in our backyard is the bane of Louis's existence. It's beautiful, but it sheds huge waxy leaves and these grenade-like pods all over the place twice a year.

"I'm bushed, actually. We were up late. I think I'll eat and take a nap."

"There's some leftover takeout we got last night if you want," Mom says, shielding her eyes from the bright sun. I can't tell if she's doing it to get a better look at me, or what exactly she'll see if she does.

"Thanks. I'll be fine." I start to head to the house. I need my bed so bad.

"Well, Mercy and Dan are coming over later tonight to do some grilling and take us on a spin in their new electric car. We'd certainly love it if you—"

I lift my hand and keep moving, because there's no way I'm hanging out with Louis's geeky friends, even if I didn't have another party tonight.

"Thanks, but Grier and I've got a sleepover. It'll be fine. I just need a quick nap."

"Okay, honey," Mom says.

"We'll be out here if you need us," Louis adds.

I don't turn around, and I don't say anything back. I just make a beeline for my bed, and pull the blanket up and around me without even taking off my suit.

Mom's hand on my back wakes me up. My room is much darker than it was when I got home.

"Brynn?"

"What time is it?" I roll over and try to find my clock. But apparently when I plopped down, my head was facing the bottom of my bed, so now I'm all twisted around.

"It's almost eight."

"Shit. Really?"

"You've been sleeping for hours. You feel okay?"

I sit up. "Fine. Van's just upping my drills in prep for State. And there's a shave meet coming up."

She sighs. "I just don't think you're getting enough rest, honey. Maybe you shouldn't—"

"I'm fine, Mom. Just a later night than usual."

"Well, I don't know if you should go out again tonight then."

It's in me to tell her she wouldn't even know about my plans tonight if Grier hadn't ditched me this afternoon, but it's not worth it. She made it clear a long time ago that she's only interested in playing mom, not actually being one.

"It's cool, Mom. Tonight's just some girl's birthday. A little sleepover. Nothing wild."

"You always came home so exhausted after sleepovers. Remember that one of Kelsey's? That meltdown you had? I always had to brace myself for a tantrum when you got home from kindergarten, because they never gave you enough of a nap."

"Well, I just had a huge one, so I should be fine." I smile even though all I want is for her to get out of here.

She puts her hand on my forehead. I force myself to not jerk away.

"Well, you're a little warm, but I think it's from sleeping. The Flytes are downstairs. Come on down and say hello."

"I've gotta text Grier, see what time she's coming over." I start untangling myself from the bedding.

"All right then." Mom sighs. "Remember, there's extra chicken if you need it."

"Thanks, Mom." At the sound of the word *chicken*, my stomach makes a demanding noise. I realize I came straight home and went to bed, without eating a thing. "I'll come down in a minute. Just let me wash my face."

"Okay, if you're sure you're all right."

"I am."

She leaves but doesn't close the door, so I have to get up and do it for her. I'm still groggy from such a long sleep and am absolutely ravenous now, but first I have to find my phone. When I do, I've got three texts from Grier. The last one says she's already on her way.

18

THOUGH THIS PARTY'S MUCH GRUNGIER THAN LAST NIGHT'S, IT certainly isn't mellow. High school kids from all over ramble through the house, while stoner college girls and their greasy-haired boyfriends lounge by a giant bonfire in the back. Grier and I have heard about these parties—run by the two college dudes who live out here, and attended by anybody who hears about them and wants to go—but we've never come out. It's a long drive, mainly, from her house. And we've never really wanted to before.

Gavin, however, must've been looking forward to the opportunity to run into so many of his old friends now that he's back in town. He high-fives and chest hugs nearly twenty different people as soon as we walk in, including a couple of leggy girls who look like they want to practice some things they just read about in *Cosmo* on him. While he says hello, Grier holds on to his arm and tries to glare toughly, though it only ends up making her look like one of them: jealous and possessive boy-crazy girls who always make parties like these extra-uninteresting. Already I want to leave. I poke Gavin hard in the middle of his bicep to get his attention.

"Where can we get some drinks?"

"Keg's in the kitchen. Come on." He holds one arm over all of us, pointing, and pulls Grier closer to him with the other. Squashed up beside him, she gives me a grateful smile. The girls in short shorts melt into the crowd, and I glare at the back of Grier's head. Gavin hasn't said, or done, anything to indicate he even remembers last night in the hall, so I don't know whether to be wary or irritated or relieved or what.

At the kitchen door, you can see the wear and tear these weekly shindigs have taken on the house. Even if the two yahoos who live here bothered to clean up between party weekends, it would still be one of those dinge-colored homes built over thirty years ago that needs much more than a coat of paint. The kind Mom and Dad and I used to live in, before. Tucked into the elbow space between the sink and lower cabinets is the keg, and we move in the direction of the people grouped around it. Behind us the rest of the counter juts out to divide the main part of the kitchen from the breakfast nook, where there's a rowdy game of Beer Pong.

"Oh, yay!" Grier bounces on her toes and claps her hands. "I want in."

"You suck at this game," I remind her.

She scowls. "Not once I get warmed up."

Gavin laughs. "Maybe you should just watch for a minute. These guys are pros."

"What, you don't believe in me?" She pokes him in the ribs. He pretends it hurts then does that lip-bite smiling thing that she must think is sexy.

"You need beer before you can Pong," I say, rolling my eyes. Standing around, watching people bounce a ball into a cup is even less of my idea of fun, but I push deeper into the crowd around the keg and grab three cups from the towering stack on the counter. I waggle one at Gavin, making a question with my eyes. He nods an emphatic and grateful yes. Grier smiles at me. I smile at her. We both smile at Gavin.

It's going to be a long night.

About a half hour later, it's clear that no amount of warming up is going to help Grier with Beer Pong. Gavin and I stand together by the wall, watching her fail and then fail again, both of us laughing and then trying not to laugh when she looks to us for encouragement.

"You can do it, baby!" Gavin shouts, hands cupped around his mouth. When he drops them back down, one clearly rests on top of mine. He doesn't move it, and I don't move either, not because I want to be touching him necessarily, but because he so clearly wants to be touching me. Immediately I know he remembers everything about grabbing me last night, whispering huskily in my ear. The center of my fly heats up, sending prickles out through the rest of me. I'm not sure whether I should move or hold still.

The decision gets made for me when Gavin starts clapping, after the guy playing Grier gets bored by her continual, giggly missing, and has begged his friend into the game instead. Grier pouts and crosses her arms, but she must realize how drunk she's getting because she does relent. She looks ridiculous and stupid, and she thinks she's having a good time. Meanwhile I've sipped down only about a third of the way through this first beer, even though it's Saturday and I don't have practice tomorrow. I don't intend on sleeping in another bathtub again. Or on that fleabag couch, either.

"Come on, let's get some air," Gavin says, hooking Grier under his arm again like she's some adorable package.

I stride ahead, imagining what I'd do if he reached out and touched me right now. Even though we're several feet apart, it's almost like I can feel his hand on my back as we go through the screened-in back porch, where a bunch of kids are staring into their own or one another's phones. We move out into the wide expanse of lawn closer to the edge of the lake, where the bonfire's happening. We sit down together in the grass, just beyond the circle of people up close to the fire. I can't tell if it's on purpose or just the way things work that Gavin ends up between me and Grier.

The fire is leaping and golden, and the kids in front of us are only tall, dark shadows against it. We're close enough to be warm, but not hot. It's dumb, I know, but I can't help checking to see if there's a fire ring. Things could get out of control very quickly with a bunch of drunk kids around, so it makes me feel better when I see cinderblocks half-buried in a circle around it.

I'm about to ask Gavin if he came here a lot when he was in high school, both to be lewdly funny and because it's awkward for none of us to be talking, when Grier goes, "You two are the best," from nowhere.

We look at her. Her face is amber from the glow of the fire, and she's propped on her elbows in the grass like a little kid. She sits up and reaches across Gavin to squeeze my arm.

"Gavin's only been here a week and I feel like we've been together forever," she coos. "I could stay here into infinity. This fire. So nice. You two." But then she jerks her head up from Gavin's shoulder. "You need to be nicer to each other, though."

She's in the let-me-tell-you-how-I-really-feel mode she gets in that means "superdrunk." We haven't even been here for an hour, I don't think.

She pats Gavin's face with sloppy little slaps. "Why aren't you nicer to my friend?"

He smiles down at her. "You're goofy. Brynn and I like each other fine."

I remember his hand on my hip, his mouth so close to mine. Not even twenty-four hours ago.

"No, you don't." Her blurry eyes roll in my direction. "Why aren't you nicer to Gavin? This is the first guy I've really liked." She leans to pat me, too, but swoops in a little too far and almost falls into Gavin's lap. I have a feeling Gavin and I are about to have to be plenty nice to each other as we hold Grier over the lake while she pukes her guts out, but I just smile at them both in a way that I hope hides the anxiety rising in my chest.

"See?" She points a finger in my face. "You don't deny it, do you?"

I don't know where she's going with this. She doesn't know where she's going.

"I just don't know him as well as you do, so—"

Gavin's elbow bumps mine.

"I just want us all to be friends," she slurs. "I want everybody to get along."

"We do get along, bratty." Gavin grins at her. "Look at us, here, hanging out. It's all good."

She sits up straighter, pulling her eyes into focus. "No, you need to hug each other."

Gavin looks at me.

"I mean it. Hug like friends."

She crawls over Gavin and into my lap, draping her arms around my shoulders and pressing her face into my chest.

"See? Friends. Brynn and I have been friends since I was fourteen years old. Isn't that amazing? All my other friends are bitches." She giggles. "All they care about are their phones and shopping. But not Brynn." She gazes into my face for a moment before her eyes drift closed. "Brynn doesn't care about anything." Giggling again. Then she sits up and crawls to the other side of me, opposite Gavin. "I mean it. I want to see you hug."

Now I'm the one biting my lip, but when Gavin looks at me, I just shrug.

"Okaaaay," he says, reaching around me to half-assedly cup my shoulders in the crook of his elbow. It's such a lame, wet-noodle move, I figure he doesn't remember hitting on me last night. These stupid gestures I've been reading tonight are all accidents. Because if he does remember it, clearly he feels it was a terrible mistake, since he's in love with Grier now or whatever. After four days. God. They're both idiots, but so am I.

Grier smiles. "Now kiss and make up."

Gavin and I talk at the same time.

Me: "What? No."

Gavin: "You're drunk. Come on. Let's go walk it off."

She scoots away from us. "You kiss and make up, and I mean it. I don't want you two fighting."

"Grier, we're not fighting. We don't have anything to fight about," I tell her. "You're being ridiculous."

"Then how hard is it?" Before I know it, she's back over to me, grabbing me by the shoulders and planting her mouth on mine. It isn't a quick little peck, either. She stays there ten, maybe a dozen seconds. "See?" Then she looks at Gavin proudly. "See?" she reasserts. "It's nice." Her hand is still on my shoulder. The other reaches out to him. "Come over here. It's nice." She kisses me again. This time the barest tip of her tongue brushes the underside of my top lip before she pulls away. She's smiling. Her hand gently kneads my shoulder. I have no idea what's happening.

"Well, it does look pretty nice," Gavin says, turning more in my direction.

That full mouth of his. That wry, wry smile. Before I can find a way to tell Grier she's just drunk and she needs to sleep it off—before I can decide if that's not true and I really want to kiss Gavin—he's got his hands on my ribs, mouth on mine. It's soft and sweet, at first, like Grier's mouth, and I think the whole thing's about to be over when things get hotter, making me realize with clarity that Charlie is only a mediocre kisser. In contrast, Gavin's tongue knows exactly how and where to go, and mine is answering back. If I were standing up, I think my knees really would buckle. I pull back only when I realize I'm gripping the back of his head with my hand, digging my fingers into his hair.

I expect Grier to either applaud or else fly into some kind of territorial rage at both of us, but neither of those things happen because Grier hasn't even seen. Instead she's crawled away a few feet and is hunched on her hands and knees, tossing up her Beer Pong dinner onto the grass.

Gavin and I look at her then each other. Because the rest of my body's coursing with wicked adrenaline and lust and I don't know what, I do the thing I know how to do best: take a deep long breath through my nose. Blow it out, slow, through my mouth. Back to the discipline. Whatever it is that's happening right now, it isn't the boss of me. Besides, Grier needs to get home, pronto.

Without much protest from her, we get Grier inside and clean her up, both of us holding her over the bathroom sink while I wipe her face and her chest with a cool wet cloth. Gavin keeps looking at me, wanting to say something or maybe even kiss me again, but I frown in concentration over Grier.

There isn't any discussion of whether or not we're staying.

"You okay to drive?" Gavin asks me.

I nod, serious. The cup of beer I'd only sipped at is spilled somewhere in the grass by the lake, and I'm fine to drive. I haven't felt more alert all day, in fact: strung tight to every little thing. I hope my face tells him not to ask me anything else as we steer Grier to the driveway. She manages to walk with us out to her car but crawls into the backseat and lies down immediately.

Because of me, because of Grier, because of whatever, we're silent in the car. Gavin checks back on Grier, mostly to make sure her head's turned to the side so that if she pukes again, she doesn't choke. *She's not going to be sick again*, I want to tell him, but his attention on her is better than on me right now. Because if he looks at me again like that, I might just stop the car and kiss him.

It's when we pull into Grier's palm-lined circular drive that he breaks the steely silence: "Man, that was intense."

I check the backseat. Grier is definitely passed out, but still.

"Get out of the car, at least."

While we do, I picture him grabbing my arm and pulling me to him, but he doesn't. I go around to the front of the car and lean against it, crossing my arms and staring into the lush greenery that is Grier's well-landscaped front yard.

Gavin stands beside me. Not close enough to touch.

"Now do you see?" he says, quiet.

"Do I see what?" Breathe. Breathe. Breathe.

"What I said last night."

The automatic mode the breathing helps me get into, plus the time spent dealing with Grier and the drive, has made me steady again. I snort.

"Do I see that you're playing two friends against each other? Sure, I see that. Pretty good convo for the boys back at school, I'm sure."

"Goddamn." He shakes his head.

"What? It's not like that's not what's going on."

A sigh from him. "I'm not playing you. That was all Grier back there."

"Oh, and I'm sure it was so hard for you."

Again the laugh, the shaking head. "You're too much."

"For you? Probably."

"You know, I really don't get you. What do you want, for me to stop hanging out with her? Because it doesn't really seem like you do."

I shrug. "Do what you want. I'm not in the habit of snatching up my friend's sloppy seconds, if that's what you're thinking."

"So I might as well just keep on fucking her is what you're saying." His voice is trying to be as mean as mine.

"She seems to enjoy it."

"Oh, believe me, she does." As if that's supposed to make me jealous. I smile a little in the dark.

"Great, then."

"I just don't see why we can't—" He leans in, bumps his shoulder against mine. "I mean, it's not like she and I said we wouldn't hang with other people."

I smile.

"I'd like to point out to you that Grier is my *friend*. Besides, like Grier says, I don't like you that much."

He growls and comes at me with that deliciously full mouth

of his, but now I'm expecting it and I dodge out of the way, laughing at him. He grabs for me, but I run around to the other side of the car, giggling.

"Come on." I open the back passenger door. "Let's get her inside and into bed."

When I start pulling on Grier's ankles, she groans and flaps at me with one hand.

Gavin moves me out of the way to lift her all the way out. She flings her arm around him and snuggles into his chest.

"Okay," he says, like there's been no pause in the conversation. "Obviously, I'm just going to have to win you over so bad, you're willing to break some rules."

I laugh again, low, reaching for Grier's purse in order to hide the look of victory that I can feel on my face.

"Yeah, well"—I blow out a long, slow breath—"good luck with that."

19

MONDAY MORNING, FOR A MINUTE AFTER THE ALARM, MY LEGS don't want to move at all, and I'm not sure I'll be able to get out of bed. It freaks me out so bad, I push myself up forcibly onto my elbows and shake my head a few hard times. Finally my feet slip from under the sheets and onto the floor. It still takes me another thirty seconds, forty-five, before I stand up to go pee. When I'm done I sit back down on my bed and stare at the floor for probably five minutes, thinking about nothing. Well, not nothing. About Gavin texting me thirty times yesterday after Mom picked me up from Grier's. I'd crashed in one of her guest rooms while the two of them curled up together. They were still asleep when I left.

I didn't realize he'd been messaging me at all until we got

home from the cemetery, when I already had about sixteen of them. They kept coming all day, even when I was at Charlie's for a while before dinner:

> i like camping.
> i know how to make a good quesadilla.
> i can type with my eyes closed. sort of.
> my roommate calls me vinny.
> really, he does. & im not italian.

Stupid things like that—things I don't get why he thinks would make him likeable. I didn't respond. Well, except after that first one, to find out how he got my number.

> g still passed out. i found her phone.

And then:

> where did u go?
> we cd make pancakes. if u know how.
> u don't seem lk the cooking type tho.

The idea of him looking through her phone—at her contacts, her photos, maybe even her e-mails—felt strange and weird, and the torrent of texts get a little annoying after a while, but I didn't mind that he woke up and wanted to find me. The last text came in at 12:46 a.m.: ok good night see you at the pool.

Now I just drop my phone in my bag, pull on shorts, and shove sneakers on my feet. Mom and I washed all my suits yesterday, so my gear is ready to go. Downstairs, Louis waits with his coffee and a protein bar for me. I pull a ball cap on, low.

"Let's go," I say to Louis.

Routine.

It's halfway through first period when my breakfast finally hits my bloodstream and my brain wakes up more. *Kate*, I think. Kate and her date. My sluggish body straightens up a little. I blink to attention. I wonder how it went.

First, though, there's Charlie to deal with. He'd texted me while I was at the cemetery yesterday too, in the midst of Gavin's bombardment. It was weird seeing his number there in the middle of so many from Gavin: still want to study?

So I went over. We hung out. I halfheartedly listened while he explained some of the major points in the last article we were supposed to have read for Conflicts, and then halfheartedly made out with him after that. It wasn't because I was thinking of Gavin, really, or wishing Charlie was him. Instead I wondered if Charlie could somehow tell I'd kissed another person. If Gavin had left any kind of mark on me. Charlie and I haven't talked about not seeing other people, but with a guy like Charlie, you just know. Surely he's assumed the same thing about me. And I haven't given him any reason to think I'm not, so far.

I left early. I couldn't even stand him unbuttoning my shirt much. He was perplexed, of course, but said he'd see me tomorrow. Hoped I'd get enough rest. He smiled when he kissed me good-bye. I couldn't get out of there fast enough.

Now, headed to our lunch table, I have to arrange my face for him again for a different reason. Because it isn't just Charlie at our table—it's Ethan, and I think his girlfriend, whatshername. Another girl from the school swim team too, maybe named Nala? Nora? I'm not sure.

"Hey," Charlie says, all cheerful and proud, showing me his friends.

"Hey." I bend down and kiss him quick, since that's what he wants me to do. For his friends to see.

"So, you remember Ethan. And Maria."

Ethan nods. Maria nods. I nod back.

"And, hey, we know each other already. On the team? You're Brynn, right?"

The N girl has stood up to shake my hand, all bright and preppy and nervous. Brown ponytail. Brown eyes. White T-shirt with light brown stripes. She doesn't say her name, which is annoying because why would I remember some random girl on the suck team? Luckily, when she starts taking apart this complicated bento box with her lunch in it, I see her name written on the bottom of one of the compartments: Nora. There's a little pop of satisfaction in me that I was right.

The rest of us get up to get our food: me and Charlie to the salad bar, and Ethan and Maria to the sub and sandwich line.

"So, what's that about?" I try to say it light.

"What do you mean?"

"We just haven't had lunch with your friends before."

He raises one shoulder, quick. "I wanted you to myself at first. But now that I really know how awesome you are, I want to share you with my friends." I can't see his face, but I can hear how happy he is. I drop a pile of shredded beets on top of the other stuff on my plate and don't say anything.

"Is that okay?"

I think. It isn't okay, though I can't really say why not. Only that, before Charlie, I didn't do lunch with other people. It was too distracting, all their boring stories and gossip and dumb jokes and playing with their food, cracking one another up over nothing. I'd go to the library. To sleep, mainly, but also to look at back issues of *Entertainment Weekly* to keep me up on all the movies and TV shows I'm too tired to watch. Sophomore year I used to hang out with some other girls in my English class, but they kept inviting me to sleepovers, shopping trips—stuff I couldn't do with them because of club practice. So last year I found myself a new drill. And then, a month ago, I guess, I found Charlie, which apparently now means more than just him.

"It's fine," I finally say.

I've reached the end of the salad bar. But I don't want to go forward.

"Look," he says, balancing his plate in one hand so he can turn me to him. "I know you think the guys on the school team are cheese, but I promise, going through puberty really has chilled a few of them out." He's trying to make a joke, but I don't bite, so he switches gears. "Polo, Ethan is my best friend. I can't not hang out with him just because I want to be with you, too. I thought this way we could—"

"I know."

"So, what?"

I look at him. At his earnest face. It really is sweet, the way he wants me to be in his life. And something about it, about him, makes me think I could tell him the real truth: that I know none of this is going to last. That I don't want either of us getting too tangled in each other, because when someone leaves—and I am going to leave—there's a big freaking hole in your life that you can never, ever get over, even if someone else steps in to fill it. When your dad is gone—no matter how many conversations you've had about how dangerous his job is—he's gone, and when your mom flips out because of it, you can't get her back either. Friends don't stay friends when you have to change schools. Eventually everyone disappears. So it's better to depend on yourself and your system, because if you don't have something to keep you afloat, you're going to find yourself at the bottom of a dark sea pretty darn quick.

I've never said this to anybody, but the look on Charlie's face—that's what I want to tell him right now.

But it would be too much. For both of us. So instead I tweak my mouth into what I hope looks like a small smile.

"Maybe I just wanted to relish you by myself a little longer, is all."

20

I SURVIVE LUNCH. CHARLIE'S RIGHT THAT ETHAN IS FUNNY, and watching the two of them riff off each other for half of lunch makes me see both of them in a different way. More sparkly or something. Warm. Maria's got tears going down her face, she's laughing so hard. I don't know; it's fun. When the bell rings, Nora leaps up and gives me a girly little hug, and Ethan, predictably, says maybe we should all do something this weekend. Charlie's happy. I'm fine. I kiss him quick on the cheek and say I'll text him after practice.

Then there's Spanish to plod through and finally Enviro and Kate. I speed walk to class, getting there early and looking up every time someone comes in, wanting to see her expression: not just about the date but about what it was like in Stats with him this morning too. Kate's face broadcasts every tiny emotion, often several at once, so as soon as she comes in and I get a glance—

"It was great, wasn't it?" I say.

She's flushing, smiling, eyebrows up in this-is-crazy doubt and maybe a little surprise. I clap my hands.

"And class today? What happened?"

"He said hey to me."

Nails up in her mouth. I'll tell her to quit next time.

"And?"

"And I said hey to him."

"And?"

"He asked me how the rest of my weekend was, and I said fine."

"Oh my god, Kate, you're killing me!"

She smiles, baffled. "What do you want me to say? You're the expert. I don't know anything about all this."

"Well, did he ask you out again?"

"He texted me Saturday. Said he wondered if I'd want to go see anyone else playing there sometime."

"Well, that's good."

"Today he asked me what lunch period I'm in."

I brighten. "That's very good!"

"But we don't have the same, so . . ."

"That's okay. This way he can miss you, wonder what you're doing."

"Oh yeah, because going to a PETA meeting is so mysterious."

"He doesn't know it isn't!" My voice is so squeaky, Chu glances up from her desk. I lean in closer, my hand on Kate's arm. "He wants to see you, that's for sure. And I'm assuming you like him, right? Golf shirts and all?"

"Oh, I almost cracked up when I walked into the coffeehouse. Because he really had on one of those plaid cowboy shirts. I am not kidding."

"So he didn't pick you up?"

She shakes her head. "My parents insisted Mom drop me off. But he did get to bring me home."

Which means maybe they kissed, but I can't ask because the bell rings and Chu moves over to the board. After class, as we move down the hall though, I grill her about the entire date, and how they left it.

"The thing is, I don't know when we're going out again, or if," she says as we take our seats in Conflicts. "He didn't say anything that meant this weekend for sure, but since I already said yes I'd like to go sometime, does that mean he assumes I'm saying yes to this weekend? I know you'd tell me not to ask him, but in class today I was so distracted, not being able to figure it out."

"You have to wait."

"I know, but what if he was just being nice and he didn't mean it, and here I am waiting and waiting. . . ."

"So you don't wait."

She doesn't buy it. "Right, I don't wait. I already checked my phone at lunch, which I never do, in case he'd somehow texted me."

I think of Gavin's slew of texts over the weekend. How I wanted to sneak in the bathroom and turn on my phone after lunch today too, but Charlie's friends had thrown me off, so I had to run to my locker between fourth and fifth instead. Plus, it would've been stupid.

I shake my head, resolute for us both. "He talked to you in class. That's enough. He needed to see how you'd react today, whether you were still interested. Believe me, he'll text you. I bet as soon as school is out."

"But what if he doesn't?"

"There could be a couple of reasons. You don't have any way of knowing what they are. The key is, you cannot initiate anything. This is like a game of Chicken or a staring contest. You cannot be the one who flinches, because then you'll both know you broke first."

"If I really had a good time, though, and truly want to go hear some music with him again, can't I—"

Woodham stands up. Time for class. I shake my head firmly at Kate before she turns around to pay attention.

"Ladies and gentlemen, I have a special announcement for you all today." He leans over his rickety wooden podium, looking over his trendy glasses at all of us. "After seventeen years of teaching, I've decided to try something a little different. Though grading your essay exams is truly the light of my life, it's become plain to me, after reading your last papers, that there is more work to do before I send you off to your more advanced classes next year, not to mention college."

My shoulders sink. Paper. That was one of my Ds. With lots and lots of Xs from Woodham's green pen.

"So in lieu of an essay exam, this year your entire exam grade will be determined by your final research paper, which will be our primary focus—save this last section on the Arab Spring and current events that are the result of it—for the remainder of our time together. Now—"

He goes to the Smart Board and projects a list of paper requirements. Everyone takes out their notes, including me. Fuck fuck fuck paper fuck. I cannot do this. He knows I cannot do this. Not just because I don't have time, but also because I really can't. I can talk a good game, but writing isn't one of my strengths. Five nondigital sources. Correct works cited. Critical analysis. Compelling conclusion. I take a deep breath and try to slow my heart, but even I know the breathing doesn't always work when you are officially freaking out.

Class is a blur. I write down what Woodham's saying, his advice about research and how we'll be spending time in the library, but my ears are full of white noise. *Paper paper paper!* screams behind my eyes, even with them pressed closed. I try to visualize the pool, slow down my breathing, but the water just becomes a sea of books with me trapped underneath them.

After class I leap out of my desk. I need to be swimming. Swimming I can actually control. But first Kate grabs the back of my hoodie.

"Hey, are you all right?"

I keep moving out into the hall.

"Crazy, right? Woodham changing things up like that at the end? Those flash cards I've been working on all semester aren't going to be very helpful now."

She's trying to read my face, figure out what's up with me, and be friendly and funny at the same time.

"I'm sure you'll be fine."

"What do you think about a topic?"

"I don't know. And listen, I've got to get to practice."

I walk faster.

"Hey, I know why you're freaked out," she calls behind me.

I spin around. "Oh, yeah?"

She closes the distance between us before she talks again. "Look. It's not like I haven't seen your tests. It isn't like you study. We all have to pass this paper to pass the class. I owe you for helping me out with Connor, so if you need some coaching for this, I'm—"

"I don't think even you can help me."

Her hand flits in the air, brushing off what I just said.

"You'd be amazed how easily a paper writes itself once you have good source material. Really. We can brainstorm a topic tomorrow in the library. I already have an idea of what I want to write about, so I can do a little research on my own ahead of time tonight. Really. It'll be fun."

My panic won't subside. "I'm telling you, Kate, I have no idea what to write about. As you pointed out, it's not like I've really absorbed much of that class."

"You know more than you think, right? You helped me see that, so I'm going to help you. No arguments. Now, get to practice. Think about anything we've covered this semester. Just let the stuff float around in your mind like historical soup for right now."

"You're nuts."

She makes a goofy face. "So are you, so there."

I watch as she turns back down the hall, toward the bus pickup.

"Thanks, I guess," I finally say.

She raises a single hand. Like it's nothing. So I start walking to the front of the school, to Louis, and to the pool where maybe I'll feel like it's nothing too.

One, two steps into the glow and gleam of the pool, then a deep inhale of chlorine, and at first my head does clear. My shoulders straighten out and my abs tighten, which makes my spine elongate—all my muscles lining themselves up for the next two hours, excited like horses before the Derby. That's until I see Gavin talking with Shyrah and Andy on the bleachers. He's leaning back on his elbows, broad chest in plain view. When Shyrah looks up and waves, Gavin sees me too and straightens up. A secret smile crosses his face. Grier is nowhere. But she's usually late. Thing is, I wasn't anticipating seeing him without her around too. I'm not ready for this yet.

Andy lifts a hand in greeting. "Hey, Brynn."

"'Sup."

I turn away from them to stick my hand in the pool, pull up a palmful of water to smooth over my hair before I pull on my cap. My legs and pits are itching—hair growing back between shave meets—but I force myself not to scratch. I work my cap down over my head instead, smoothing out air bubbles that aren't there, blocking out thoughts of Saturday that shouldn't be there either. I swing my arms around in their sockets, rotate my elbows. Anything to not sit down. The texts were one thing—those I could just ignore. Him, here, looking at me like that at the pool? I didn't prepare myself for the next move, and I'm too shaken up from Woodham's class to think about it now.

Fortunately, Grier rushes out of the locker room, and for a second her giant sparkling smile washes me in relief. Grier will be funny in practice today. Grier will make me laugh during the logic puzzle and make faces at me across the lanes when she's burnt out—Grier will help punctuate the drills with silliness, and by the time practice is over, I'll be wiped of everything else, charged and ready to go see Charlie, lie down with him and forget the rest of everything until tomorrow.

Except, of course not. It isn't like that anymore. I remember as soon as she wraps her arms around my neck and gives me a grateful hug.

"Oh my god, this weekend. I'm so mortified about what happened. Like, on a gigantic level. I'm so sorry I did that to you. I feel like a punk."

"I told you, you suck at that game."

She's still holding on to me. "I know. And then I was barfing and passing out. Gavin said you both had to carry me to the car. I don't really remember. I'm sorry about all of it. I promise, next party, I will not bail on you again like that. Next time we'll have fun, right? You are really, truly the best."

My face is calm, stone. I make myself hug her in return.

"I think Gavin's mad at me about it, actually," she goes on, lowering her voice. "I wanted him to stay Sunday afternoon and watch a movie with me, but he said he had to go and get some stuff done. I thought he might come back over later, but he said he was tired." She bites the edge of her lip. "Do you think I should go over and apologize again? He hardly texted me at all yesterday. I didn't bug you about it because I know you had to go to—you know."

I ignore her lame excuse of my being at the cemetery as a reason for not texting me. Pretending to think, I look over at Gavin for the first time since I came in. He's watching us. Smiles again at me. I squash the warm swirls that sweep under my ribs.

"Well, you two have been at it pretty hot and heavy lately. Maybe a little space isn't terrible. At least for one practice."

"But what if he thinks I'm a total ass now and never wants to see me again? I mean, this guy, he's amazing."

I put my hand on her shoulder and level my gaze at her. This is real and true advice: "Don't prove him right by being an ass right now."

And, at least during practice, she doesn't for the most part, though I don't really pay very much attention to either of them.

Instead it's four 50s, free, building speed each time.

Kick for two hundred.

Pull two hundred more.

That's the warm-up. Then pep talk, logic.

Back in the pool—two 50s, fast.

One easy.

Three 50s fast this time. Faster than the others. More.

One easy. Blank now. Breathing.

Four 50s, fast as fast as fast.

Three hundred free, easy, to cool down a little.

I don't stop during any of it. Van tells me the next drill, and I don't look to either side. I hardly notice Megan in the same lane as me or whether I've lapped her. I am push and cut and tight and breathe and push, and then I'm draped over the lane divider, breathing more. Van squats down, palms my skull in his hand. We are both pleased, for the same reasons, and also different.

21

AFTER PRACTICE I WANT TO EAT THREE HAMBURGERS AND slide into bed for the rest of the night because I'm still a little burned from the weekend. But as yesterday's awkward time with Charlie proved, even after an hour of rolling around with him, I sleep like a baby. Plus, since some of the kids from school swim team will go to State, and Charlie hopes to be one, his practices have intensified too, which means I can crash with someone who understands how tired I am and why. When I get to his place, we barely even talk. He heats up two heaping bowls of leftover pad Thai, and we flop on his giant leather couch. His sisters, Chloe and Cinnamon, are splayed on the floor, eating Fudgsicles and watching some cartoon with talking fruit in it. I don't know if it's because it's truly funny or we're just so tired, but Charlie and I can't stop giggling. My feet, where they're entwined around his calves, glow warm. For a minute I think I could stay here forever.

After two episodes though, we hear Charlie's mom's car in the driveway. His mom with her cheery questions. Probably she'll invite me to stay for dinner.

I put my empty bowl down on the floor. "I've got to go."

Charlie's surprised.

"I know," I say, seeing his face, "but we've got a paper for Conflicts, so—"

His brow furrows. "Not the exam?"

I shake my head. "He changed it this year."

He gets serious. "What's your topic? Why didn't you say? I can—"

His mom comes through the door. "Well, hi there, Brynn! What a pleasure."

There's a tug in my heart.

"Hi, Ms. Berger. I was just telling Charlie I'm afraid I have to run. Big paper for my history class."

She looks at me, eyes scrunching a little. "Dr. Woodham's class? Why, I'm sure Charlie can help with that. You loved him, didn't you, Charlie?"

This is getting worse by the minute. I can avoid my own mom by escaping to my room, but Charlie's—not so much. And I'm just not into the family thing.

"Thanks, but my friend Kate's going to help me out," I

explain to them both, rushing. "I just remembered, I need to look at my notes. See if I get any ideas."

"Topic wise, keep in mind that Israel–Palestine will get you more points with him," Charlie says, though he also looks confused about my leaving. It's annoying and overwhelming. I so cannot write this paper. I don't need him reminding me or making me feel bad about it.

"Let me look things over, and then maybe tomorrow we can talk about it," I murmur as his mom moves past us to say hello to the girls. "I mean, I appreciate it, but—" I'm off the couch, going for my shoes.

"You don't have to go. We can—"

"Yes, Charlie, I do need to go." My voice is so sharp, his mom and sisters look up. "Okay?" I try to be softer.

He heaves himself off the couch, taking our bowls to the kitchen, and sighs. "Do what you have to do then."

I don't know why I don't want to leave with him irritated, bad as I want to get out of here. I shouldn't care. But I follow him into the kitchen anyway, put my arms around his waist.

"I had fun at lunch," I say into his back. "And this was really nice."

He doesn't move. I rub my pointy chin into a knot of muscle just under his shoulder blade—the swimmer's spot. I press hard.

"Ow." But at least he turns around.

"I just need to do some of this on my own, okay?"

"Yep."

"We can talk more about it at lunch tomorrow."

"Sure."

I sigh. "I don't know what to say."

He squeezes my hands. "Just say good-bye for now and go work on your paper. I should probably do some stuff anyway. So once again you're the tough one, all right? You win."

"That isn't—"

"I know. It's okay." He rubs his brow with the heel of his hand. "Let's just both go do some work, all right?"

I hug him close, pressing my cheek against his chest. I need to leave, need to go, absolutely right now. But I linger there, my ear on his heart, listening to it beat steady. Strong. Alive. Here with me.

"Okay," I finally say, pulling away.

22

ONE SEVENTEEN IN THE MORNING. I YANK MYSELF OUT OF sleep—heart pounding—a rush of heat sweeping over me. I'm awake. It's okay. It wasn't real. I sit up. The dark of my room shifts into recognizable shapes. I take a deep breath, hold it, and let it out. The images of my nightmare dissipate, but not enough: Dad and me and one of my middle-school girlfriends on a drive in the country, listening to music and being happy. We follow a curve in the road, but it becomes broken gravel, rocks, and then deep black sand. The tires get stuck, spinning. Dad presses the gas harder. Black sand is flying all around us. My friend is panting with panic. The car sinks deeper into the sand. Dad starts to sweat, like someone's pouring a bucket of water over him. The engine makes terrible noises. We sink lower and lower. The dark sand presses against the windows, and they begin to crack.

I've gotten used to these since he died. Before, I would go into Mom's room, get into bed with her. Most of the time she was out so cold, she never noticed I was there until the morning, but that didn't matter to me. I just needed some company. In the morning she would wake me up, stroke my hair, and ask if I was okay. She never made me talk about the dreams—just knew I'd had a bad one. Maybe she couldn't handle it, but that didn't matter then. I liked that she didn't need to know the details.

Now, of course, it's all different. After another minute or two of blinking in the dark, feeling my heart slow and the fear unwind from my veins, I go downstairs silently, turn the TV on, and pull a blanket over myself. It'll take some time before I fall asleep again. But I figured out a while ago that TV company is better than none.

23

WHEN KATE AND I GET TO WOODHAM'S CLASS THE NEXT DAY, there's a note on the door instructing us all to go straight to the library. The dream last night was exhausting, and the TV kept me awake more than it helped me sleep, so most of the day has sucked. I made myself smile and pay attention to Charlie and his friends at lunch again, which I guess is a thing now, but it's made me even crankier.

"So, don't you even want to know?" Kate says as we head back down the hall. "I mean, I'm trying to be cool over here, but you're barely saying anything and I kind of can't stand it."

"Hmm?"

"Uh, class today?" She's blushing. "I just thought you might want to know if I talked to Connor or not. But, I mean, it's not that big a deal—"

"Oh gosh, no. I mean, yes, tell me. Sorry, I'm fuzzy."

I knock myself on the side of the head, trying to be cute. But *fuzzy* is an understatement. *Fuzzy* implies warm. Something you'd want to cuddle down into. Not shards and spikes and a cloud of choking dust.

She looks at me from under those bangs, unsure.

"Seriously. I mean, I'm assuming something's happening this weekend."

That smile. "Yes."

She tells me about the acoustic performance he invited her to at a place where you can order dinner, too. Where John Mayer got his start, like anybody cares. I nod, I listen. She says he's going to call her after school, and I tease her about being old-fashioned. She blushes again. It's fun. Fun enough, I guess. She likes him. He likes her. He's still being a grandpa about it, but maybe that's what nice guys do. I feel a small smile, thinking of Charlie, and maybe trying another date with him, but then—

"Wait, say that part again?"

Kate's face clouds. We're at the library now, where almost everyone else is scattered at tables in the front. She speed walks us over to one in the back and then ducks down in her chair so low, it's almost embarrassing.

"I said I just hope he doesn't expect me to, you know. . . ." she whispers.

"What, kiss him?"

"Shhhhhhhh. God." Her whole face is red. Even under those bangs. "It's not that. It's just, you know, the other."

I can't help laughing. "Do you mean you haven't—?"

"We'll talk about it later." She points at Woodham. "Pay attention."

I blink, not believing, and then not believing my own disbelief. Of course Kate hasn't done it. Who on Earth would she have done it with? Her parents had to drop her off at their date last weekend. From what little I know about Kate, it wouldn't surprise me if this were the first time she's ever gone anywhere alone with anyone, especially a guy. Maybe he's even the first person she's kissed. It makes me picture my own first kiss, back in—what? Seventh? That guy Gordy. The back of a dark van, coming home from a meet. I guess my little girlfriends had been in awe about it when I told them, though it hadn't felt like anything special to me. Kate's going to need some serious advice.

A thought of Gavin swims up in my brain, but I clamp it down. It's important to at least fake-listen as Woodham explains the importance of actual texts in this paper. But as he goes on and on, I start to I feel more and more like a bag of sand again. Black, gritty. The kind that sticks to your skin and gets in your throat. When he releases us to do our research, I want to lie down in one of the aisles and cover myself with a pile of books. Maybe the information will just seep through my skin.

Kate's all business though, pulling out her binder and

smoothing open a blank page in her notebook. "So, what did you decide you want to focus on?"

Clearly, Connor and necking are not suitable topics.

"I don't know," I grumble. "Civil War?"

Her brows come together. "Well, that's an awful lot to cover."

"Doesn't that mean it'll be easier?"

"Um, you can't exactly cover the entire Civil War in one eight-page paper. Woodham'll knife you for even trying."

"Woodham's going to knife me no matter what."

Her face is both impatient and determined. I watch, unmoved, as she writes out a list, trying to show me how one preps for a paper like this. My eyes are almost too bleary to concentrate on her writing. But we have to have a subject turned in by the end of class.

"What about this one?" I point. *Death of Lincoln.*

Her eyes light up. She goes on for almost five minutes about some actor and his crazy multiple-murder plan, the long chase through the country to catch him and what it meant, the first president to be assassinated.

I try to blink away the gritty feeling. "You seem pretty charged about the topic. You should take it."

"I already have most of my paper outlined already. I just think it's interesting."

Of course she has her paper outlined. "Sure. Conspiracy. Revenge. Sounds great."

She grins. "And then he really gets it in the end, too. You'll love it."

Twenty minutes into trying to read some of the books Kate's pulled for me—way more than I need or could even carry—I hear the low, distinct *bzzzzzz* of my phone vibrating in the side pocket of my bag at my feet. I look around to make sure no one else heard it, especially not Woodham, who'd take my phone away from me just for having it on during school hours. I pretended this morning to forget to turn it off, figuring my battery might die anyway, struggling to find a signal under the iron curtain that surrounds our school. I wasn't really hoping Gavin would text—I just wanted to know if he did, so I could keep track and not be caught off guard like yesterday. If things are really cooling off between him and Grier, I need to be ready for what might be coming next.

Even just the small idea that maybe he's finally made a move again does make feigning interest in Kate's research a little easier, I admit.

24

EXCEPT, WHEN SCHOOL'S OVER AND I'M FINALLY ALLOWED TO check, the message isn't from Gavin. Instead it's some spam text from our cell phone plan telling me about some stupid upgrade. This means the last thing I heard from Gavin was his text after practice yesterday: **you are a powerhouse.** I got it when I got home from Charlie's. Two minutes later there was also a message from Grier saying Gavin still hadn't called her and what should she do. I ignored Gavin and told Grier to keep ignoring him, too. It wasn't out of any kind of strategy, either—I was just still feeling strange about how I'd left things with Charlie.

Now it's almost a relief to see this new message wasn't Gavin. Because it means he really is a puss. Obviously, he's already tired of both Grier and me—which I knew was going to happen the whole time. All it took was a few hours of ignoring him. That it happened so fast is a little disappointing, but it doesn't matter. Now Grier can get over it, and we can go back to normal. Dealing with Gavin in the pool for the rest of the summer will be the same as not dealing with him at all. I was right, and it didn't even take that long.

When I get to practice, though, Grier's actually on time—and standing right next to Gavin, chatting with the other guys on the team like they're all best pals. Like my teammates weren't all chicken of Gavin and his friends just last week. Like I didn't firmly tell Grier to ignore him not even twenty-four hours ago. It's more than annoying—it's weak, the way she has no discipline. I twirl my arms in their sockets and smooth my cap, trying to remember some of the Lincoln crap I was reading up until the last bell, instead of wondering what happened to the girl who once took a dump in her prissy neighbor's yard just because I dared her to. Trying not to feel the sand underneath my eyelids. Definitely not being joiny-joiny with all those hose-weeds over there.

Grier's palm on my back makes me jump.

"Hey"—she laughs—"you okay?"

"Sure. Just focused. Only a few more—"

"Yeah, yeah, I know." That mocking, bored tone in her voice. "Blah, blah, blah, qualifiers. But listen"—her eyes go over to everyone on the bleachers—"my dad's coming back into town this weekend, so I thought I'd invite some people over before I'm quarantined, you know?"

Both she and I know that even when both her parents are in town, she's never really quarantined in the way the rest of us are, but it's clear all she wants is for me to say yes. Without meaning to, I glance over at the boys on the bleachers. Gavin is very not purposefully looking over at me and Grier, and is instead pretending to be very interested in whatever boring-as-hell story it is Shyrah's trying to impress him with. Gavin's spine is straight, his abs all fully sucked in so that you can see every hard-earned ridge. Thighs clenched, tendons taut. I think of my hand in his hair, his mouth on mine. All those texts. I should say no. I should just go home, work on this damn paper. It would be better for all kinds of reasons. But then his shoulders shift and his chin tilts and I catch him sneaking a sideways glance over.

Still, I can't make it easy.

"I've got a big paper for Conflicts, so I don't know."

Grier's eyebrows pull together. "You don't really care about that, do you?"

"No. But my teacher does. It's basically the whole exam. If I fail, I have to take summer school."

"Well, that would suck. But you could come over for just a little while. Eat something, hang out. You could work on your paper later. Relaxing after practice a little might help, right?"

Van comes out of his office then, and Grier gives me a panicked look.

"I just thought," she says, "some kind of thing with everyone would make things . . . I don't know . . . less serious feeling for Gavin or something. More fun. But it won't be fun if you're not there."

I feel my mouth wanting to twist into a smile. I have to fight it. Hard. "Okay, but I can't sleep over or anything. It can't be that wild."

"Oh, no," she promises, doe-brown eyes wide. "Dad's back from Japan around nine, so everyone has to be out. It's just a get-together, you know? Just everyone hanging out for a little while. Gavin can drop you home."

I shouldn't be doing this. I'm way too tired today, and the stuff about Woodham's paper isn't exactly a lie. But Gavin is fully looking at us now.

"Okay. But you have to be the one to explain to Louis."

She squeezes my hands in hers. "You're the best."

You'd think the water would be the last place a bunch of swimmers fresh out of practice would want to be, but at Grier's it's as if it's the only place we can be comfortable with one another. I'm surprised at how many people are here: Gavin-Linus-Troy, of course, and Shyrah and Megan, but also Dylan, Sam, Kelly, Lucy, and Siena—people we hardly talk to or hang out with at

132

all. I don't know what Grier told them, or what she told Louis about this afternoon either, but it doesn't matter. Louis just said to be home at a reasonable time. I texted Charlie and told him I was working. He texted back that he was proud.

Now the twinkle lights are on, but it's still not dark out. Nearly every floatie and toy in the Hawkins's collection is in the pool, and I bump into one from time to time, lying across one of my own, eyes shut, half-dozing. There is laughter. A bag of marshmallows is being passed around, though Grier can't get the fire pit going, and no one feels like helping her. Someone jumps into the pool with a loud splash. The water ripples around us. I open my eyes as Linus pulls himself up onto the end of my floatie, a joint between his lips. His wet fingers pass it to me. I've had some of that lemonade and vodka stuff Grier mixes in big pitchers for gatherings like this, but I didn't mean to drink any. I was going to have water. But then a Solo cup was in my hand and I was twirling in the pool on a giant plastic doughnut and, well—

Linus laughs, his eyes happy slits. I take a drag and then see my hand passing the joint back to him. This will be a funny thing for us all to talk about at practice tomorrow. It was actually a nice idea. It feels good to just lie here, floating, surrounded by hazy laughter. I picture Charlie and his sisters, asprawl in front of the TV. It might be fun if he were here too.

I fan my hands in the water, pushing myself closer to the

edge of the pool, the Grecian tile spinning dolphins at us in a turquoise cascade of jumping delight. Megan kicks past me, her bottom breaking the surface and bobbing like a plastic toy someone could shoot and win. There's another splash. The Jacuzzi bubbles somewhere to the right. There is a person or two in there. Drifty faces. Grier is laughing, hard, in the shallow end. The light is perfect. Someone leaps off the diving board. Someone else hollers, "Sharks and Minnows!" and we divide into teams, moving toward separate ends of the pool. Somewhere in the back of my blurry brain, I think maybe, if it could always be like this, I might not mind people so much.

I slide off the floatie and shove it out of the pool. Before long, I'm in the dark-blue deep end, clinging to the gritty edge, more than a little buzzed now, but trying to look ready to launch at our attackers. I hear myself call words of encouragement, see Shyrah's proud shining head four feet to my right. I know he can make the entire length of this pool in one breath. I think he is a good teammate. I should be nicer to him. Someone screams, "Go!" and there is a bunch of splashing. I'm not sure where the No Man's Land marker is. There are bodies swimming past me, and I dive, trying to grab. They may be my own teammates. I don't care. I'm laughing underwater. This is so nice. Hands are flailing, faces wide and open above the water. The light continues to dim, almost in a steady stream, like you can see it disappearing. The air above the pool is so warm. More laughing.

A shriek. Then Gavin swims by me, flinging water off his fore-head, not even looking at me. I go under again, aswirl in the bubbles he makes, waiting for him to pass by me, but without warning, he's turned around and his warm hand is on my knee, then above my knee, sliding into the curve of my thigh. Up, higher, gripping me firm. Unapologetic. Not hesitating. Warm and knowing and utterly there.

I kick—once, twice, forcing us apart. He breaks the surface at the same time I do. His teeth are straight. His hair is dark and sleek. His cheekbones hang droplets off their sharp edges like Christmas tree ornaments. My crotch is burning where his hand kneaded it. He's just a few feet away, treading water, face happy though he's not looking at me again. It's like it didn't happen. But I'm on fire. My legs kick themselves in circles in the water, over and over, not sure what to do. I reach for the edge again, clinging, letting my body drift down, down. Hanging there, useless.

It doesn't take long for the game to lose its fizzle. A bunch of us head into the Jacuzzi. Someone passes water bottles around, a universal signal that things are winding down. It's still not dark yet, but it's about to be, and we all feel it. Partying for us is a little like sprinting—a big, huge burst of energy and then, ugh. A few people go inside to change. Even the music quiets. I look around the yard.

"Where's Grier?"

"Probably getting bent in half by Gavin upstairs," Troy says, laughing. It shocks me, something so vulgar coming out of a guy who looks so gentle. It's even weirder when Linus gives him a high five, but I know they're both right. I feel mad again all over. Grier said it wouldn't be fun without me here, but what she meant was no one would come if I didn't. And then she couldn't hook back up with Gavin.

"What time is it?" someone wants to know, changing the subject.

Kelly stands up then and asks does anyone need a ride. Without thinking, I raise my hand. Kelly doesn't drink, but she doesn't judge, either, and she always insists on driving people home if they need it, no matter where they live. Since she goes to my school, we live pretty close, so I don't feel bad about it. I need to get out of here anyway.

"Get some rest," she tells me when she drops me off, serious. "You look like you could use it."

I thought I was doing a good job of faking it in the car, but I guess not. As I say bye and go into the house, part of me wants to prove her wrong, stay up awhile, but that would mean joining Mom and Louis for their dessert, and I really don't think I can fake it with them tonight. Not when my eyes are rimmed red from weed and exhaustion and I still feel a burning handprint between my legs.

So after the obligatory "How was your day?" and "Fine" and "Thanks for letting me go to Grier's," I grumble something about getting some reading done and take a plate of dinner up to my room. They both look concerned, mixed maybe with some disapproval, but they can't argue with me much if what I'm doing is homework—the main thing they're always harping on me about. Of course what I really do is eat and watch a few videos on YouTube. Around nine I get a text from Grier: **making up iz awesum!!!** There's a photo attached, but I don't need to look at it. A glance at my notifications tells me she's already tagged me in a bunch of pictures from this afternoon too. So. Happy-go-lucky Grier again. Friendy friend friend blah blah blah, all kissy and made up with Gavin, fuck lord of the universe. I put my laptop onto the floor and curl under the covers.

Kelly's right. I do need some rest. Tomorrow—I need to be back on my game.

25

NO DREAMS, ONLY SLEEP. IN THE MORNING I'M BACK TO NORMAL.

Wake.

Pee.

Dress.

Breakfast, and the game with Louis in the car.

School.

School.

Charlie, lunch, his pals, whatever. Charlie asks me how the paper's coming, and I even remember one or two things from what I read yesterday.

More school.

Then Kate and some light teasing about this weekend. Enough to keep her glowing, anyway. Woodham's stupid lecture on works cited. We'll be in the library again tomorrow, getting shown some database by the librarian.

Then, finally, practice.

At the pool, everyone who was at Grier's is giggling and sly-eyed, mooning over what fun we all had in our little social club yesterday. Which means instead of tuning out with earbuds, priming myself for what I know needs to be a hard workout, I have to stand there and chitchat, too, because otherwise Grier will think something is up. Which, fine—I know how to play this. I hold my face in a way that suggests I'm listening, though I don't say anything myself. I move my face in a smile when it's expected. I can't look at Gavin, because as soon as I hear his voice, all I can think about is him grabbing me in the pool yesterday. I know it's important not to acknowledge that gesture even in the slightest, so I hold still. I keep everything in me even. It's hard to not see him though, since Grier's standing right next to him, bumping him with her hip from time to time, but even more important than being unfazed by yesterday is making regular friendly eye contact and laughing with her.

When Van comes down, I realize my jaw's clenched so tight, my teeth hurt. I take a breath, try to relax.

I am normal, aloof. I am what I always am.

I get in the water. I swim.

I am fast, faster, fastest.

I get it done.

• • •

In the car on the way home, I can feel the tightness in me finally ebbing a little when a text *brrrrrings* in. Inexplicably, a burst of anger crawls up my neck and behind my eyes. Gavin needs to just fuck off, leave me alone, and go waste his time on Grier since he loves screwing her so much. But I know if I actually said all that, he'd think I cared what he does. Besides, it is amusing how much my ignoring bothers him. Couldn't even stand it one whole day. Someone needs to tell him to quit being so pathetic.

But the message isn't from him. It's from Charlie.

polo, ok if we don't hang today?

I pause, trying to picture what I'll do instead in the time between now and dinner. I see myself riding bikes with my dad. Watching him repair the lawn mower for the sixtieth time because we couldn't afford a new one. Him teaching me how to play poker so that I could sit by him and not be bored when the fire station guys came over for hoagies and beer.

ok. I type back.

I wait. Louis makes some comment about my popularity these days as we get out of the car. He sounds impressed, glad for me, but I barely register. What's wrong with Charlie that he doesn't want to hang out, especially since we didn't yesterday?

After how chummy I've forced myself to be with his pals, he can't think there's anything wrong with me. Besides, I need him. I need him to clean my palate from Gavin, so to speak.

you ok? I text, after he says nothing.

yeah it's no big deal. ethan's just over.

I picture them watching TV or playing video games, with Cinnamon and Chloe laughing at their jokes. Being goofy. Being friends.

tell him hi. have fun.

I am fine about it, I am. Charlie's just doing—whatever it was he did before we started hanging out. He needs to see his friends. It's totally normal. It's his routine.

make it up friday? he finally says.
sure, I agree, not understanding any of this.

With little else to do, I try reading more of the books Kate found for me on John Wilkes Booth, but it's hard to focus on anything. My eyes keep blurring and trying to close. I read several pages over and over. Downstairs, at dinner, which I have no way of escaping, I try to recite some back to Mom and Louis. I know from experience that the weight of silence with both of them really is worse than the effort of talking. But I can't keep all the dates and names straight. I switch to trying to explain this other whole book that focuses on the significance of the Civil War in terms of how it shaped current politics, with a lot of speculation about where we'd be if Lincoln hadn't been killed and—I don't really know what I'm talking about.

"Sounds really interesting." Louis nods, scraping his plate clean. Trying to help me out a little.

"You know there are several battle sites around here," Mom says cheerfully. "Maybe we could all go—"

"'Fraid all I'm going to have time for is practice and this stupid reading until the semester's over," I say, getting up and clearing their plates.

They nod and *mmm*, proud and understanding, which drives me crazier than usual for some reason tonight. To force myself to be calm, I stay and load the dishwasher, and even wipe the counters.

"Thanks, Mom," I say, heading back to my room. Doing the dishes—pushing myself through something I don't want to do—has given me an idea, and it doesn't involve reading any more of this boring crap.

kate its b. I text. I'm not sure if Kate really pays attention to her phone or if she's used to anyone texting her, but it's worth a shot.

To my surprise, she answers pretty quick: brynn?

yeah. i can't do this, I tell her.

????? she asks.

these books r killing me.

go slow. take notes. draw pictures if you need to.

I roll my eyes. annowhatevrs due friday, right??? I ask her.

just the 1st 3.

i can't read all this by then, I insist.

just summarize.

I growl and want to throw the phone.

you've read all these tho, right?

This time she takes a little longer to answer: not the swanson.

"Come on, Kate. Get with me here," I mutter out loud to the empty room.

so you cd help, right? explain in english?

it's really not that hard, she says.

Okay, fine then. Make me bring out the big guns.

how r you feeling abt fri? I ask.

my annos are done.

no i mean connor.

Again, another break before she answers. And when she does, she calls me direct.

"Do you think I'm stupid?" she says as soon as I answer.

"Of course I don't think you're stupid. I'm the one who's stupid here. And I'm asking you to help me."

"I know what you're trying to do."

In spite of myself, I'm impressed she's calling me on it.

"What am I trying to do? All I'm trying to do is make a fair exchange. You know stuff that I don't know. I know stuff that you don't. We trade, and it's not that big a deal, right? You like this guy, don't you?"

She humphs. "So far, anyway."

"And he likes you. You want to keep it that way, right?"

"Are you trying to say that he won't like me if I don't help you?"

"No, God. I'm your friend, Kate. Jeez. I'm just saying I could tell you a few things that would make sure and keep him interested."

"Brynn, I'm not going to do your work for you. I offered to help, but . . ."

I grip the air in front of me with clawed hands and shake it.

"I'm not asking you to do my work for me. I'll write the summaries. I even know how to do the citations right and everything. You saw me take those notes. All I'm saying is, can you please help me understand what these books are even about? Just describe them to me in normal language? Because I could read until two thirty this morning and still not figure them out. And I have practice tomorrow, and you don't know this, but I'm getting ready for a really big meet. Teachers like Woodham don't understand what it's like. They think we're just a bunch of dumb jocks. But you're exhausted after two hours of practice, and by the time you get something to eat, which is absolutely necessary—and I mean, like, totally vital—it's already almost seven and in order to get a decent sleep you need to be in bed by ten thirty at the latest, and what about the rest of your homework, huh? It's not like Woodham's the only teacher I have."

I've gotten a little dramatic, I know. But sometimes the best way to get what you want is to keep talking until the other person agrees, just to make you shut up.

"I don't know."

"Kate, please. I really need your help." She probably doesn't know how honest I'm being.

"I have homework of my own, you know." Though I can hear she's giving in.

"I know. I really do."

More quiet. I wait.

"I'm not doing this for any kind of . . . sex advice," she finally says. "That was pretty low of you, to be honest."

I laugh, surprised. "I know. I'm sorry. It was the only thing I could think I might be able to offer. To make it worth your while."

"You can make this worth my while by writing a damned good paper and at the same time keep up your practice so you can win the championship or get into the Olympics or whatever it is you're trying to do."

"I will, I promise. This will help so much. With all this reading, I can't—"

"Hey, I already said I would help you. You don't have to keep laying it on."

I hope how funny and snarky Kate can be is part of why Connor likes her.

"You're a good person, Kate." And I mean it. "Really, thank you."

"Save it for when you get an A on your annotations, okay? But listen, I better go. First though, how did you get my number?"

"We exchanged them at the beginning of the semester, duh. You said maybe we could study together sometime."

"That's right," she says. A beat, then: "I just didn't think you'd really programmed me in."

I don't know what to say to this.

"Well"—she sighs—"I'll see you tomorrow. But keep reading a little, okay? You'll still need quotes for the paper."

I tell her I will. And at first, I do try—I really do. But the reading is long and boring, and I'll have time to do it over the weekend. In order to not be a total slack-off, I make myself do a few math problems. Also, I finish our vocabulary assignment for English so Mrs. Drummond can stop giving me the evil eye every time I walk in the door. There's actually a good word in there: *vituperate*. To abuse someone with harsh language. I can think of more than one person I'd like to vituperate right now.

When Mom and Louis come say good night, it surprises me that it's ten already. I wash my face and get in my pajamas, but it's like my post-practice drowsiness has worn off: My mind's not ready to go to sleep, even though I know my body needs it. Once in bed, I pull my laptop back off the floor and spend another hour pulling together a collage for Kate made from stupid dating advice and GIFs I find. (Well, not all of them are stupid. "Not insulting yourself" is a good one she could probably listen to.) I'm not doing it because of the bibliography thing—I'm really not. Instead, picturing her reaction tomorrow, I can't stop myself. Against my better judgment and my discipline, it's something I honestly want to do.

26

IT'S ONLY BECAUSE I'M UP WORKING ON THE KATE PROJECT that I hear the quiet ping coming from my bedroom window around eleven. I look up to where the sound is coming from, confused and startled, and wait. About five seconds later there's another one, harder and louder. So loud, I imagine Mom and Louis can hear it from their bedroom downstairs. My heart rate accelerates. Someone is definitely throwing rocks outside.

But I can't open the window and lean out, a la *The Notebook* or whatever dumbass movie, because Louis always sets the alarm before bed, and it goes off if you open the window without turning the alarm off first. I know this from experience.

Still, I go to the window and peer out.

Gavin.

I feel both pissed and a little victorious. As I'm standing there, another rock hits so hard, I'm afraid it may chip the glass. I signal to him that I'll come out, but I don't know if he can see. I hurry downstairs as quietly as I can and punch in the code for the alarm, praying Mom doesn't hear it but getting my excuse ready in case she does.

Opening the front door seems impossibly loud, though I also know from experience that if Mom doesn't hear the alarm code deactivating, she won't hear this. One step, two, and I'm outside. Gavin's standing in the driveway, looking between my bedroom window and the front door, poised with another pebble from the driveway in his hand, just in case.

"What the hell?" I spit. "This isn't 1950, you know. Or even 2004 or whenever you first heard of that trick."

Thanks to the streetlamp, I can see his smile, though most of his body is in the shadows. "Yeah, but it still works, right?"

It's not cold out—it's not even cool—but I feel my nips harden under my cami, anyway. Suddenly I'm very aware of the thinness of my boxer shorts. I cross my arms over my chest and try to look pissed.

"Whatever. What are you doing here?"

"I was bored."

Somehow, in that small statement, he's crossed the lawn and is now standing in front of me. I can't actually smell Grier on him, but I imagine I can. I glance at the house in case the hallway light's been flicked on, which means Mom really is awake. I'm both relieved and a little disappointed to see that it's not.

"Look," I whisper to Gavin. "This is more Grier's bag than mine, you know? I actually have parents who still believe in things like groundings."

"Aw, they can't ground you." He smiles. I realize he's not totally sober.

"I told you anyway"—I toss my head, trying to feel as confident as I know it makes me look—"I'm not interested in my best friend's sloppy seconds."

I sidestep toward the driveway, where it's harder for anyone to see us from the house, but not so far that I trigger the automatic outside light. Somehow, in my doing this, Gavin also closes the distance between us. He's here, over me, hands on my hips like that time at the party. Like they were meant to be there.

"Oh, you're not sloppy. And you're definitely not second, either."

I keep my voice steady, mean, though my pulse is rapid. "Doesn't seem to be the case, since I guess you're back with Grier."

He doesn't say anything. His face doesn't even shift.

"What's up with you and all this partying anyway? I thought you were in summer training."

"That's the operative word," he drawls. "Summer."

"Yeah, well, some of us are still in season."

He laughs. "Yeah, I know you're seasoned."

"What's that supposed to mean?"

"I just think you know exactly what you're doing."

He leans in then, kissing the sharp curve of my collarbone. His hands slide down just enough to make my hipbones pop out from the elastic edge of my boxer shorts. Goose bumps rush along every inch of my skin, including what feels like over my face. His mouth on my neck knows all the right places. I can envision how red his lips are. I think of his hand on me, in Grier's pool.

"What are you doing?" I murmur, unable to stop myself from stepping closer to him, raising my chin so he can get at more of my neck.

"Only what you want me to." Kissing toward my sternum. His hands dropping even lower. The way he's holding his hips away from me, I know he's hard. It helps bring me back to myself, helps me get control of the heat.

"I'm not calculating anything." I make myself take almost a whole step back.

He laughs. "Okay. Like you don't like it better when I'm with her."

"I'm not sure I know what you're talking about." My pulse shifts its pace.

"Oh, sure. Like I haven't noticed how it always gets a rise out of you, the two of us together. You think I don't think about that when I'm with her?"

A curl of disgust wells in the back of my throat, even as he bends in to kiss the curve of my neck again. When I realize I've grabbed a handful of his T-shirt, I let go but don't exactly step away.

"I'm not trying to make you fuck over my friend. You're doing a plenty fine job of that on your own."

He looks amused. "Doesn't look like you're trying to stop me, either, is all I'm saying. I kind of think you want me to."

My eyes narrow. "You have no idea what I want."

"That's true. But I sure am interested in finding out." His lips hover over mine, and I really think he's going to kiss me—I picture it, us, by the fire—but then just like that, he steps away, just some guy in jeans and a T-shirt, laughing at me.

"Good night, champ. I understand you've got a big meet coming up. You better get your rest. I'll look forward to seeing you tomorrow."

He heads to his car in no hurry. I should go back into the house. I should. But I stand there, making myself watch him until he's gone. Seeing him finally leave is the only thing that quiets the heat in my shorts and the steam I think might be coming out of my ears.

27

AS SOON AS MY ALARM GOES OFF, *WIPED* IS THE ONLY THING
that comes to mind. I hit snooze three times, which I hardly
ever do once. I could stay here. I probably should stay here. I
need to be sharp, rested. These last few practices before next
weekend's meet are no joke. But then I remember Gavin last
night—that cocky laugh. I can't back down, pussy out. I cannot
let him faze me. Plus, it'll be fun to show Kate the collage.

Downstairs in Louis's office, though, right before we have
to leave, the freaking printer is out of both red and yellow ink,
so Kate's poster comes out all weird. There's no time to change
it and try again, and I'm so tired and so annoyed—still flustered
from Gavin—I almost cry. But instead I suck in a breath, press
down the frustration, and go grim-faced to the car, because I

still need to face Woodham and the library and the homework I actually did for once, plus Kate and those summaries, and on top of that, figuring out what the hell is wrong with Charlie and why he didn't want to hang out with me yesterday. Not to mention practice later, and how to deal with Gavin and Grier. God damn it. I hate people. I hate people so much.

When Charlie sees me in the lunchroom, though, it doesn't seem like there is anything wrong with him. His smile is just as happy as it always is. Like there wasn't anything weird at all about him turning down an afternoon make-out in order to hang with Ethan. Like I don't partly blame him for my inability to sleep, for me still being up when Gavin came over, for my light being on, for Gavin being able to figure out so easily which window was mine. Though I half-dozed through my first three periods, now my eyes are grit and I feel heavier than I did getting out of bed this morning.

I stiffen my spine, clench my butt. I can't let any of that rule over me now, and I definitely don't want Charlie to think I'm uncool about him hanging with his friends.

"Where's the gang?" I try to say brightly, though it doesn't come out near as friendly as I mean it to.

He reaches for me. "Off campus, I think."

I stay standing, beside my chair. "Did you want to go?"

"There isn't really enough room for us in Maria's car, and I know they're not totally your thing anyway."

Why he has to say something like that, I don't know. I've been totally fine with them. Jesus.

"I like those guys plenty, it's just—"

"Maybe I wanted some time with you, huh? You let a guy just have that?" His eyes are sparkly. "Come on. Let's get our food."

I pile on potato salad, even extra chicken breast this time. Boiled eggs. Anything that will give me some energy. While we eat, I decide to tell him about Kate and Connor and the collage I did for her last night so I won't just sit here and bitch, letting anything about Gavin slip. After I explain the whole thing about Kate, though, surprisingly Charlie gives me a couple of good, from-the-source pointers to add in. Real boy-perspective stuff I hadn't thought of.

"Of course, she should also make sure and talk about her period." His face is completely serious, though he's having trouble keeping the laugh out of his voice. "If there's any way to work that in there."

"Oh, absolutely," I deadpan back. "Even if you're not on it, you should let him know where you are in your cycle, right? Plus the heaviness of the flow?"

He nods but doesn't even hint at grinning. "Make sure to clarify whether you're a pads or tampons girl, too. It really helps set the tone for the rest of the relationship."

That he's so unflinching about it is the part that cracks me up. That or plain old delirium. And once I start laughing, something unhinges in me and I can't hinge it back. I sound like a hyena. Which, of course, Charlie eats up. The rest of lunch, we think up the grossest, most disgusting things Kate could do on their date this weekend. Everything that comes out of Charlie's mouth is hilarious. I'm like Maria, laughing at Ethan with tears streaming down her face, right there in the cafeteria. I know I sound crazy, but I can't stop.

That is, until I say something about pubes in the teeth and Charlie says, "For the record, I'm not interested in that tomorrow night."

Then the giddiness spirals out and away from my body.

"Tomorrow?"

Charlie twists his mouth. "I just thought, we've all been practicing so hard, and I know heading into the end of the semester is rough, so maybe we'd, you know, go eat a mess of food somewhere. Catch a movie. It can be just you and me, or we could group it. Maria usually has people over Friday night. Chinese food. It's fun."

Just briefly, a protest rises in me, thinking of the routine, which group hangouts are definitely not a part of. But then my veins turn to lead. My weekends aren't about Grier anymore and the escape of her place. Especially not since, apparently, she and Gavin are back to being whatever they are, either regardless or because of me. The thought of it makes me feel even more weighed down, more tired. Tired of him. Of it. I am plain, stupid, cold-dead tired.

"Whatever you want to do sounds fun." Between my ears, my voice sounds like it's coming from underwater. "Maria's, even. If you want."

There's a bag of sand on my shoulders, a chain connected to the table, pulling my whole body down, down to rest on its greasy surface. I squeeze my abs hard, keep myself up straight, but right now it's hard to see the point. Even with Charlie's big happy smile, beaming back at me.

I absolutely cannot stay awake in Spanish.

It's nearing the end of the day, though, and I've got to be on it for practice, so between there and Enviro I detour around to the cafeteria to buy myself a Dr Pepper. When it clunks out of its slot, I immediately press the cold can against my closed eyes. Then I pop it open and down the whole thing on the walk over to class. It makes me thirty seconds late, since I stop outside the door to make sure I don't have any last burps to let out, but already the rush jetting through my bloodstream feels better. I don't like to rely on uppers like caffeine or those 5-Hour Energy frauds, because they are unhealthy crutches, but this week's been a little weird. Today can be an exception.

It gets me through class, at least. I'll probably need another one on the drive to practice, but this way, I can keep my head up.

"You okay?" Kate wants to know as we walk to the library for Conflicts.

"Just tired. I was up late last night."

"You've seemed tired a lot lately."

"No, I haven't."

She shrugs.

"I was up working on something for you, actually." Deflecting the subject.

"Oh?"

The frustration of this morning, that fucking printer, washes over me again, though.

"It's funnier if you see it in person. So I'll save it."

"Well, thanks, I think. Here."

She shoves a handful of papers at me then, ones she's been clutching since we left Chu's room. My summaries. I'd forgotten them. But taking just one glance, I can see she wrote over a page for each book.

"Um—thanks." I'm so grateful and relieved, it's hard to look at her. I feel embarrassed she's done this for me.

She doesn't know what to say either, so we go into the library, carrying our silence between us. I know to tuck those summaries away as fast as possible, hide them until they can be copied over in my own words. Kate and I sit together at a table, but she takes out her notes and pretends to read over them. So she doesn't think I'm a total wasteoid, I sit up straight during the demo from the librarian, take some kind of notes, and try to listen, but even with the extra caffeine, I'm still so heavy. But this time, I'm pretty sure it doesn't have to do with being tired.

As I arrive at practice, the chlorine smell reaches out to snap me from my drag, but it's not working. I pad down the hall in my bare feet past the locker room to the regular women's bathroom, where it's more private. After changing, I splash water on my face, slap my cheeks—hard—three times in a row to bring the blood back. I glare at myself in the mirror, flaring my nostrils. Kate. Gavin. Charlie. School. Whatever. It doesn't matter. This does.

I suck in a hard breath and then clench every muscle in my body as tight as I can. I count slow to sixty. This is ridiculous. This is pathetic. I have a couple of late nights, a couple of weird encounters, and I'm all droopy like a baby. There isn't time for this. More important, there isn't a need for it. It's self-indulgent, and it's weak. Never breaking eye contact with myself in the mirror, I reach my arms over my head and bring my hands together as though preparing for a dive. Breath still held, I watch the hollows between my ribs stretch out, the rock-hard curves of my shoulders and pecs stiff and solid. You could bounce quarters off every inch of me, anywhere on my body. Fifty-nine, sixty. I let out my breath slow, unclench everything. A wave of ahh washes over me. I'm better.

Hell. You could bounce quarters off my fucking heart.

• • •

After warm-ups, I make sure to sit next to Grier, on the other side of her from Gavin, but still friendly. Pals. I don't have to. I could just sit wherever and probably neither of them would care. But as I told Kate, there's power in getting through something you hate.

We have only three more hard practices, including today, before our taper week next week and then the big shave meet Saturday and qualifying for State, which, more importantly, means making National Cut. Still, it's a big meet for everyone, so now Van's even more into confidence, self-care, and smart carbs than usual. I feel myself zoning out. Maybe I should've gotten that second Dr Pepper.

At one point Grier elbows me, but I don't know what it's in reference to. I elbow her back anyway, as though I've understood.

When Van's done, he orders us to the nearby weight room so that we can do dry lands. Everyone groans, and there's some under-breath cursing. Of course, this is exactly how I feel too, but again I keep my face still. I will be all about whatever Van needs to throw at me, at us. This tiredness is nothing. Neither is Gavin trying to catch my eye. That dumb-ass thing he said last night about me liking it better when he's with Grier.

We grab our weights and then do lunges all the way around the pool, three times, plus a bunch of rotator cuff stuff. Squats.

Side layouts. Then full-body pushups, ending with two-minute planks. Around me, my teammates are squealing, groaning, or at least breathing hard, but I keep my gaze at a specific spot on the concrete in front of me, letting my own breath out slow and even. It's hard; I won't lie. My arms are shaking, and my eyes feel raw, but I tighten my butt and push my hips forward a few millimeters farther, feeling the tautness along my whole abdomen and enjoying the burn. The hurt. I will hold this. I will hold this. I will hold it until the end.

When Van blows his whistle, I look around, still holding my plank. Almost everyone has collapsed, cheeks against the cold floor. I want to too. I want to so much. But immediately across from me, the only other person still holding his plank is Gavin, smiling at me huge.

One hundred fly, easy.

Four 75s, backstroke, on 1:30.

One hundred fly, on 2:00.

Breaststroke.

Fly again, on 2:00.

Freestyle.

Then pull kicks and buoy, ending with 200 fly.

I take it easy and slow there at the end.

Sometimes forcing yourself to relax is part of it too.

• • •

Out of the pool, I towel off and wait for Grier, just to push myself that last bit further. Van's talking to her and a couple of the other sprinters—Siena, Dylan—probably about their suck times, from the look on Van's face. Siena can barely bring her eyes up to meet his, she's so upset with herself, and Dylan keeps jerking his head in these short, sharp little nods. Grier though—Grier could care less, standing there with her hip cocked and her arms crossed, just waiting for Van to be done talking. Her cavalier attitude is even more exaggerated than before she met Gavin. Before she found something else to care about. Other teammates move past them to the locker room then emerge again with clothes-yanked-on speed. Shyrah and Linus offer me high fives. Everybody's gone except Van, the sprinters, and Gavin, who is obviously lurking, talking to ha-ha Megan. I am heavy, so heavy, but I will stand here and I will make myself wait.

"God," Grier finally huffs, coming over to me. She's yanking a towel over her head. Her buzz cut is starting to grow out actually cute. Without meaning to, I picture Gavin raking his hands through her hair, then mine.

"I can't wait for next weekend when we can all just show Van how much we suck and have it be done with. He knows I'm not going to make State. Jesus. I don't know why he keeps acting like I might."

The old, encouraging me hauls herself up, automatic:

"You're not a bad swimmer. If you actually worked at it a little—"

"As if." She glares in the direction of Van's office, to where he's disappeared. "But, hey, it's not like I'm not getting a workout anyway, right?" She smiles up at me.

Uncontrollably, god damn it, I look in Gavin's direction then yank my eyes back. More impish grinning from Grier.

I shake my head and laugh in the back of my throat in a way that I hope sounds dismissive.

"I'm surprised either of you can swim half the distance of the pool then. Since you know Van's going to ream you out, why don't you just skip practice altogether? Sounds like you need your beauty rest. And if you don't really care—"

I make it playful. I make it.

She rolls her eyes, rubbing the towel over the rest of herself. "I probably should quit. It's so tiresome how we can never have any kind of a life. Everybody had a great time Wednesday. And it's idiotic that that has to be abnormal. Linus is having people over tomorrow night, in fact. He doesn't care either. I mean, whatever. This is just basic training for them, right? So why should we push ourselves to death? I think he likes you, by the way."

It pulls me out of my thoughts about fun. About pushing.

"Linus?"

She touches her big toe to the top of my foot. "We could double-date?"

Now, now's the time Gavin chooses to come over, having apparently dismissed Megan. The way he's walking, those shoulders back, chest out, I can tell it's all on purpose. Such a fucking peacock douche.

But my timing's still nothing to sniff at either.

"Oh, gosh. I mean, it sounds fun, and Linus is nice and everything, but Charlie and I have a date." I smile up at Gavin on the last word.

"Bring him along," he says immediately, echoing my fake-happy expression. Something in his eyes, though, makes it seem like he's thinking about me kissing Charlie in all the places he kissed me last night. Good. He should be. I should be too, for that matter.

"Yeah, come on. Charlie never hangs out with us." Grier snakes her arm around Gavin's waist. I wonder if he's thinking about me holding him that way too.

"That's nice," I say, "but I think he has special plans."

"Ooh la la," Grier says, giggling. "That's interesting." She widens her eyes in a pointed way, as though we'll need to talk about it later. As though I would tell her anything these days. "Saturday, though? Again? Charlie could come too."

Yeah, right, Charlie could come.

"Gosh, I don't know how I'm going to keep up with you, Grier," I tease. Not. Looking. At. Him. Though the exhaustion really is starting to take over now. "I thought your dad was in town anyway."

She ignores my last comment and raises her hands over her head in victory.

"For once I've beaten her!"

There's no point in even acknowledging this. And I'm not sure I can stand here much longer.

"Come on, little champion." Gavin puts a hand on Grier's shoulder. "Let's go get some burgers or something. I'm starved."

She cuddles up against him. He starts to lead her away and then pauses, faking that he just thought of the idea. "You hungry too?"

"No, thanks," I say, tossing my head just a little. "You two go stuff your faces."

"Oh, we will." Gavin winks, obviously getting what I meant and flaunting it.

You do that, I think as they walk away together. *You stuff yourselves with each other until you pop.*

On the ride home, I text Charlie. It isn't the Gavin thing—it's really not—but this time I'm the one not up for hanging out after practice. That makes us skipping out on each other three times this week, which is a little strange, but there are Kate's summaries to translate into my own words, and beyond that, I seriously need some sleep, and it won't take an hour of messing around with anyone to help me get there.

All Charlie texts back, after about a half hour, is **dinner tmrrw @ maria's. shes xcited! ok?** It's the last freaking thing I need today. I didn't really mean it when I said that thing about grouping tomorrow night, but whatever. I text back, **fine** and shut my eyes. Right now I just need some protein. I need my bed.

28

IT ALWAYS AMAZES ME WHAT A DIFFERENCE SOME SOLID sleep can make in your life. Van talks about it all the time—how important it is for us to eat well and rest—but sometimes I forget. I forget how good I can feel after eight hours of sleep. It only takes one nightmare-free night or a hefty nap over the weekend before I'm back on track. I thought I was going to die of tiredness last night at eight when I crawled into bed and set my alarm for four thirty, but now it goes off and I don't even mind. I pop up right away, do my thing, and then spend the rest of the time until Louis comes down reworking Kate's summaries into pieces that sound slightly like I might've written them. I even have time to change the ink cartridges and print out her collage.

"What's this?" she says when I slide it to her in Enviro.

"Oh, just a little good-luck charm. And, thanks, too. Hey—you look really good today."

She has on makeup. Not a lot, just some mascara and maybe a little blush. Lip stain. Just enough to notice. Her hair is different too—straighter somehow, shiny. And she's wearing a scarf.

She tries not to look pleased with herself; fails. "Well, I don't want Connor thinking I can only get gussied up for dates, right?"

She wants to seem cool. She almost pulls it off.

"That's right." I nod. "But regular old slumpy Kate should still make an appearance from time to time."

She makes a noise of protest. As though she's not ever slumpy.

I toss my head. I really am back to myself. "You don't want him getting all cocky, thinking he's the cause for your glowing metamorphosis. You're just doing all this because you feel like it. Certainly not for some boy."

"But what if—?"

"I'm just saying, keep him guessing." I wink. "They like it better when they don't know exactly what to expect. Besides . . ." I think about her protesting my advice last week, and now here she is, obviously all suckered-out on him but working it. All of it having worked. It boosts me even more. "You want him to like the real you, right?"

"Lip gloss and a little hair pomade isn't enough to hide the real me. Let's both be serious."

There's the bell. The start of class.

"Yeah," I whisper, smiling, knowing what I'm about to say will make her blush. "But you'd be amazed how finally getting a little action can transform a girl. You need to brace yourself."

Woodham's apparently pretty serious about making us focus on these papers, because he gives us the whole class period to read through our other two sources—the ones with summaries due on Monday. While we do that, he collects the ones due today and grades them to hand back so that we can see where there's "room for improvement." I try to focus, but he can't seriously believe that we'll read all this in one hour. Besides, it's more fun trying to distract Kate by drawing dirty little pictures on the edge of my paper and putting them where she can see. By the end of class, she's red faced and choking back giggles, and I feel like ten thousand bucks, at least.

Woodham hands back our summaries, but I don't even look at mine. I feel great. As Kate and I walk out of class, we're both still giggling.

"You're too much," she says. "And yet"—she taps her chin thoughtfully—"I kind of want Connor to meet you. If you promise not to embarrass the shit out of me. My parents are already bad enough."

She's shy about this, so I make sure not to laugh. Still, thinking of Charlie and his friends, that party at Grier's—the one with the swim team that feels forever ago now—it occurs to me that sometimes, people can be fun.

So I'm surprised, in a good way, when I find myself echoing Grier to Kate, "Yeah, maybe we could double-date."

At practice I'm back to smoking everyone. Grier teases me about my date with Charlie tonight, about how sweet it is, and even though it's right there in front of Gavin—which, thanks a lot, dick, for insulting me in front of him—I don't bother responding to her. She can make fun of me and screw Gavin upside down ten ways to Sunday for all I care. He's still watching me when we leave the pool, and I know it. And, well, he should be watching me. Because shit, look at me. I am on fucking fire.

29

IT'S FUNNY THAT CHARLIE WANTS TO DRIVE THE THREE AND A half blocks between our houses to pick me up on the way to Maria's, but whatever. Mom and Louis are delighted. I'm still high from how great this day has been anyway.

"Why, Charlie, we never get to see you!" Mom coos, giving him a big hug. Louis shakes his hand and claps him on the back, asks how his times are looking. Both of them are treating him as if we're actually girlfriend and boyfriend, like this is just the beginning of some future they can smile into for the rest of their lives.

It makes me suddenly feel the way I do with Charlie's mom, whenever I'm over there and she starts getting all chatty. Or how I've felt before, going on dates with him: trapped and alone—pretending this isn't going to end. I plaster a fake-interested smile on my face while Charlie politely answers Louis's suck-up questions, but I can't stop staring at the picture of me, Mom, and Dad on the mantel, all of us smiling. Smiling because we don't know.

When I apologize to Charlie for Mom and Louis's annoying gushiness once we're in the car, he just shrugs it off.

"Eh. They haven't seen me in a while. And I'm a lot to fuss over."

Something about the way he says it—his jokey, unruffled smile, maybe, and my gratitude that he's so sweet and reliable—makes me lunge at him. Probably it's just because we haven't been together for several days. But, in spite of my doomed feeling just now in the living room, I take his face in my hands and kiss him with the power of my whole body. And as I do, to my surprise, the fizzy feeling I had with Kate this afternoon bubbles up again. Soon my tongue becomes his tongue and the swirling between us melts the rest. I think, *Maybe it could still be good, even if it ends. It could still be, for right now, something nice.*

"Okay, they really are watching us," he says, laughing low.

When I look, Mom and Louis, indeed, are peering out the living room window. Giddy, dizzy, powerful, I smile big, wave. Charlie waves too. He starts the car and we back out, laughing together as we go.

• • •

"I'm so glad you could come!" Maria squeals, opening the door for us. She's in a swirly boho outfit that is totally surprising, considering the jeans and scoop-neck T-shirts she favors at school. Giant hoop earrings bob beside her merry cheeks, and several silver bangles chime on her thin wrist as she leans in to give me a hug. She's like a gypsy princess or something, glimmering with color and light.

"Thanks for having me." I pat her back, a little stunned. "This is some kind of tradition, I guess?"

"Every Friday." She beams. "Unless, you know, there's a school game or something. So, it's not, like, every Friday, because sometimes not all of us can do it, or there's something going on, but, gack"—she fans her hand in front of her face in a flutter—"you get the point. Oh, this is my mom."

Coming toward us is a small, flowy woman with the exact same heart-shaped face, the same brown eyes as Maria's, only she is plumper and much more wrinkly.

"So nice to meet you. Welcome." She grips my hand in both of hers as we shake. She's wearing three different scarves, and there's a waft of patchouli when she moves.

"Everyone's in the sun-room," Maria says to me. Then, to Charlie, with eyebrows going up and down: "And Chris brought Juniper."

Charlie makes a noncommittal sound and puts his arm around my shoulders as we follow Maria down the hall, past the kitchen, and into a window-lined room full of tropical plants and wicker furniture. Ethan and Nora are there, leaning together over what looks like an intense game of War. Watching them is another guy I vaguely remember from freshman swim team—must be Chris—and the aforementioned Juniper, sitting ramrod-straight and holding a glass of lemonade like it might be poisoned.

"Ah, the lady of mystery finally joins us," Ethan says, getting up to hug me and then Charlie. Nora drops her cards and rushes over to hug us both too.

"This is going to be so fun!" she squeals, trembling like a Chihuahua. Her excitement is both off-putting and kind of cute.

"Well, you know me and Chinese food," I say. To say something. But really I'm feeling chalky white inside, looking at the card table. I haven't played many card games since Dad died. There hasn't been any reason to.

"Go Fish up next," Ethan says, abandoning War and scooping up the cards.

"Awesome," I say, shaking off my shock. "I totally rule at Go Fish."

"And then we get serious. Spades, which we're all still trying to beat Nora at," Maria says. I smile just to be polite. I used to rule at that, too. Unless my dad and his friends were always doing that annoying let-the-kid-win trick.

When Nora explains to me in her elementary school voice

that that there's actually intense scorekeeping involved and prizes at the end of the night, something in me clicks over from hesitancy to determination. Everyone else talks and laughs, barely paying attention, while I focus like my dad taught me on what cards they're asking for, what I might try to keep from them in my own hand. I beat them for several games, and when we switch to Spades, everyone can just forget about it. Doesn't even matter what the prize is—I'll be taking it.

It's Juniper's turn to deal when we hear the *beep-beep-beep* of an alarm-armed door opening somewhere.

"Dad!" Maria shouts, her face delighted. "How do the pork buns look?"

There's the sound of rustling plastic bags and a cheery hello, and then a tall, strapping, very fireman-looking guy stands in the doorway, holding his arms open, greeting us all with a giant smile. He has glasses and a gray beard, but still.

My throat goes dry. My eyes are furry and weird, and I can't breathe as I watch Maria and her mother hug him. Charlie squeezes my thigh under the table, but I jerk away involuntarily. The cards were one thing. Those I could master. This dad who looks a lot like mine, hugging his teenaged girl like that, is all way too much.

"You doing okay?" Charlie asks soft in my ear.

My eyes dart to everyone. The simple delight on their faces, the happiness around this room, the childish games. This universe I've carefully avoided so well for so long: where there's a real dad and a real mom. A real whole family.

Suddenly I have forgotten about winning.

"I'm fine," I finally whisper back to Charlie. "But isn't there anything to drink?"

His brows come together, disapproving. Before I can pretend I'm joking, Maria's mom waves us into the kitchen, where Maria's dad hands us plates and ushers us to the long, expensive granite counter laden with Chinese takeout containers. I have to rest mine on the edge of the counter just so I don't drop it. Then we're routed into the dining room, where there's a table longer than my bed. There are candles. Maria's mom sits at one end, and her husband sits at the other. Us kids are in between, like Snow White's dwarves. The dizzy feeling accelerates. I keep my eyes on my food because I can't stand seeing Maria's dad down there, though I'm not sure I can eat, either.

Maria's parents talk together about things they've read and heard this week—really sharing with interest—but they also want to hear about what we're reading, films we've seen. Everyone but me answers as though they've been waiting to be asked all night, but I can barely lift my water glass. From time to time, Maria's mom laughs in a way that wings out over all of us like a bird. At one point I realize it's over something I've said, though I'm not sure what. I swallow and try to smile back. I feel like the forks are made of paper and there's way too much light in here. Like I might not be able to stand back up.

Finally there's the clearing of plates, Maria squealing something about cheesecake. There's a chance for the rest of us to escape to the bathroom or pretend we're interested in the books lining the shelves in the den. I grab Charlie's hand and pull him into the hallway at the darkest end, by a china cabinet and the door to what is maybe the guest room.

"You having an okay time?" He rubs my arms up and down.

All I want is to kiss him. I want his hand between my legs like Gavin's. I want all this—all of it—to drop away, disappear. When I go for his mouth, though, he dodges.

"Maria's parents are a trip, right?" Hands still up and down but holding me a little bit away.

"Sure." The last thing I want to think about is Maria's parents. I push against Charlie, pressing my lips against the place where his come together: the place where he smiles. I peck at first, warming him up, but then my tongue moves in, hungry. He humors me a little but stops as the shadows change in the hall, everyone milling so happily in the kitchen. I ignore it, them, him, and grab his shoulders, pulling him closer.

"Hey," he says, decidedly stopping me now. "Are you okay? This is a little—"

"What?" I'm angry, frustrated. He needs to just kiss me now. Now, now, now, so that I don't—

"There're just"—his hand gestures down the hall—"people."

"So?" I'm still not letting go. "Don't my mad Go Fish skills drive you up the wall?" I hope he can't hear how my voice is shaking.

"They are pretty astonishing." He smiles but sidles around me, out of the corner. "But can we cool it, just for now? I mean, I like it. Just—not here."

On reflex, all the muscles in my legs stiffen, because the edges of my eyes are tingling again like I'm going to cry. To keep that from happening, I consciously squeeze everything in me harder for three seconds, four. Ten. Maybe if I do it hard enough, I'll get a cramp and can get out of here. I try to concentrate on only that, instead of being mad. Embarrassed. Irritated. Hurt. I don't want to be here with any of them.

Charlie strokes my arm again, but it's too late. I want to slap him away.

"Later, though, okay?" he says, trying to soothe me. "Most definitely."

All I can do is blink at him. Before either of us can say anything else, Maria's voice calls down the hall: "What is it, you two? Raspberry or chocolate?"

"Why not both?" Charlie says, sliding his arm around me like nothing's wrong, moving us down the hall toward Maria and her stupid fattening dessert.

"Oh, I don't know," I manage, hoarsely. "I might've already had too much."

• • •

Still, I make myself eat a thin slice, just so Charlie doesn't notice how pissed I am and then ask me about it later. More happy-go-lucky conversation happens around me, but being angry with Charlie gives me something to focus on instead of feeling blindsided by Maria's dad, and so now I'm just concentrating on bearing it, on getting out of here. When Maria gets up to clear the dessert plates, the way her father smiles and thanks her makes me want to throw something at him. Them both. I claw my fingers into my rock-hard quads under the table. I will tough this out just like everything else. We go back into the sun-room, and Ethan tallies the winners. The prizes are given out. Even though I trounced everyone, the pride I feel is gone. When Maria's mother hands me my gift certificate, I can barely look at her. At anyone.

"You okay?" Charlie wants to know when we're finally in the car together.

I nod.

"You got quiet all of a sudden. I wondered if it was weird— you know, with all the close-knit family stuff."

It shouldn't surprise me, not if I'm honest, but still I'm stunned to hear it was really that obvious. *You don't have a dad either*, I want to say meanly. But I don't. Partly because Charlie does still have a dad. Just not in the same city. Which is still a better situation than mine.

"More people than I'm used to, is all."

He accepts it. Or at least doesn't say anything else. We drive back to my place, quiet, knowing there's no time to stop and make out anywhere. Which is fine, because even being this close to Charlie right now is making me want to crawl out of my skin.

"You have practice in the morning, right?" he says, parking in my driveway.

"Eight fifteen, like always." Even I can hear how tight my voice is.

"Hey." He's looking at me. "Are we okay? I mean, are you?"

I keep staring straight, out the windshield. "Just tired, like I said."

He shifts in the seat, turning fully toward me. "Well, it was much more fun with you there. I've missed you."

I squeeze his hand, but I still can't look at him. He leans across and kisses my neck, squeezes my knee. His fingers are firm and unapologetic, just like Gavin's. Reflexively, I push my hips toward him, inviting him to go up farther. I suddenly want him to replace that feeling. Replace everything in me.

As soon as I grab his hand and press it up, though, he clears his throat and looks toward the house. "We should probably both go soon."

I don't know what's wrong with him, stopping us all the time.

"What?" he says, defensive.

I hadn't realized I'd made a face.

"Sometimes I don't get you" is all I say.

"Get me how?"

"I mean, boys are supposed to be crazy about this stuff, but you're all like—"

He laughs, embarrassed, and wipes his hand over his face. "Are you serious? Look at me." Gesturing toward his lap in a shy way. "Of course I'm crazy about it. It's just that you're tired, and it's curfew. You have to be up early in the morning, and so do I. We're in your driveway. I can't just flip you onto the backseat, Polo. I mean, I'm trying to do the responsible thing here."

I realize Gavin would flip me onto the backseat. "I know you are," I finally say.

"Look." He lets a slow breath out of his nose. "Let's just get some rest. It's been a weird week. I'm sorry about tonight. I know it was too much."

What's too much is how I had to endure all that at Maria's, and then him calling attention to it and turning me down almost within the same breath. Thinking he's doing me some kind of favor by the whole thing. I push open the car door and get out.

"Polo, wait—"

"It's fine," I say, leaning back in, though I'm not sure I can hold my face straight at this point. "I just have to go. You're right. We're both tired. Okay? I just need to go to bed. I'm sorry."

"Come over after practice tomorrow?"

I nearly scream. "Yes, fine."

"And, hey—it was awesome watching you slay everyone tonight."

My lips tremble into a smile as I shut the door and wave. I try not to rush up onto the porch while he backs up, but once I'm there I stay crouched in the dark section where Charlie can't see me waiting until he's left, and Mom and Louis can't see that I'm home, either. A place where I can hover, alone, in the dark, refusing to make a sound, refusing to shake, while hot tears squeeze themselves between my pressed-closed eyes and fall, no matter how hard I'm trying to hold them in.

30

THE NEXT MORNING GRIER, GAVIN, AND LINUS ARE ALL MISS-
ing from practice. Assholes. When I make query eyebrows at
Troy about it, he just shrugs with this pissed-off and slightly
hung-over look on his face. After Van's pep talk I pat Troy on
the shoulder, almost telling him how much better he is, being
able to party and show up for practice, but I don't really feel like
comforting anyone. Too many complicated feelings from last
night are still hovering, and I have to shake them all off. Now.

So it's just as well Gavin's not here, or Grier, either. Since
this is my last practice before taper, Van pours it on. I can tell
he's thought about how to really push me in this last hard practice, and as I go in to my third fifty, I feel a wash of gratitude.

More than that, though, it makes me want to show him that
even when he pushes me, I can push harder.

Fuck you, Grier, for not caring anymore.

Fuck you, Gavin, for trying to play with me, and her.

Fuck you, Charlie, for wanting me only in the ways I won't give.

Fuck whatever. I know what I'm capable of: this.

I go home, eat. Spend some time in front of the TV. When Charlie texts to see when I'm coming over, I beg off and say practice was vicious and has worn me out. I don't want him to ask me questions, don't want to talk about last night. He pesters me a little, but I deflect and insist I had a good time. Just tell him that I'm worried about getting enough rest and all the school stuff coming up. If he's mad about it, if he doubts, he doesn't say so. Just **okay fine**, and then that's it.

Whatever, Charlie. You can't be the one calling the shots.

Grier and Gavin pick me up for the party at 8:42. During the afternoon back-and-forth with Charlie, Grier also sent a ton of texts, half of them around the fact that she forgot I was at practice this morning, and the rest figuring out details and then her sending a bunch of exclamation points. Part of me almost bailed on them, too, after deflecting Charlie's crap. But I took a nap and woke up with a clearer head.

There are things I still need to stay on top of.

· · ·

When we get to the lake house, it's the same as last time, though maybe the music's louder. Same keg, same Beer Pong, same kids gazing into their devices on the back porch, same bonfire—same. Within ten minutes, I've filled my beer then woven a bit around the kitchen, waiting for Grier and Gavin to get involved in the Pong game—which Grier insists she's practiced for this time. As soon as they're engaged, without looking back, I head out to the bonfire.

Standing in the not-too-hot-yet night air, I get why people come here—all this beer, all this space. It's a different way of disappearing, out in this happy crowd. Trying to remember good things instead of bad, for a while I meld into a part of it, see what it's like. I stand near the fire, eavesdropping on a bunch of baseball dudes trying to tell jokes but forgetting where they are in the middle of them. Someone passes around a joint, and since I don't have practice tomorrow, I take a few hits. There's some laughing. People talking about shit I don't care about. I just sit there, listening. Drifting. A little while later this bright-eyed guy starts playing guitar, and half the people who were previously standing there head inside. The joint comes around again. I stay and smoke, smugly aware that Gavin's probably wondering where I am now. He's a dickweed, is mostly what I think. The whole point of coming tonight was to stay out of his range and watch him pretend not to be looking for me, watch him being a loser without his even knowing. I should probably keep moving in case they come outside, but the guitar guy is actually good. I sing along with him—under my breath, not loud enough for anyone else to hear—to a Flaming Lips song, and then another I recognize only part of the words to and don't know who it's by. I'm really starting to get into it, when he starts playing something slower, sweeter. The few couples around me lean closer to each other. Suddenly goose bumps race up my bare arms as I listen to the words. Without warning, I want Charlie. To tell him I'm sorry for today and how I was last night. I want him to be here with his arms around my shoulders. I want to tell him how much I appreciate his understanding, how I want to be a better girlfriend.

And then, suddenly, I want my dad. To be able to tell him about Charlie or anything else. Even Gavin, though Dad would probably kick his ass if I did.

The unbidden thought makes me take a sharp breath and stand up. I whirl away from the lake, the weed, the bonfire, the guitar. I can't sit here. I need more to drink.

I stumble a little into the kitchen, blinking from the harsh change of cozy dark to cheap fluorescent light. The laughing is superloud in here. Pong's apparently switched over to BattleShots, and Gavin and Grier aren't anywhere to be found. I find a cup—maybe it's clean, maybe it's not quite—fill it with beer, drink down half of it, then fill the rest again, hurrying. It's dumb to drink and smoke at the same time, and I'm already overly buzzed, but I don't care. I want to do something crazy or just curl up and pass out. I want to get out of here. I want—I don't know what I want; I just don't want this feeling. I move into the living room, where people are doing headstands. In the next room some girl with maroon-dyed hair has an Ouija board. I stumble, turn, and find myself moving down the hall, pausing. Trying to think. I left my phone in Grier's car. Maybe I can get her keys and ask Charlie to come pick me up. Maybe even after all of this, he would still love me, if I let him.

"There you are."

I turn. The light in the hall is fuzzy. I squint toward the voice. Gavin.

"I'm afraid there's been more Beer Pong," he says, like I didn't know. "I tried, but I couldn't stop it. You're apparently the better policeman."

"Woman," I say. "I make a better policewoman." My voice feels thick, lost.

"You're right you would."

He comes forward, hand aiming for my hip again, like it's some kind of Blarney Stone for him to rub for good luck. Somehow I know he's going to do it, and so in one fluid motion I open the door behind me, step back into the dark, away from him, making him come at me a little more. I don't know what's back there, in the room. We could fall into nothing or outer space.

But it's just an office. Two desks, from what I can see from the hallway light. Posters on the walls. Computers. There isn't much time to take it in, because Gavin's mouth is on mine.

Hands.

Hands and hands and hands. On me. Up my shirt. Down around my ass. Mine around his. We were holding beer cups before, but they're not there anymore, only this incredible heat that blocks everything else. Swirling, falling, I rush into it. The muscles of his back are like the keys of a piano I could play. His hands slide up my spine, down my chest, and over my hips, burning me up in all this orange. Evaporating. He's rubbing himself against my leg, and I try to find something I can push against. Harder. More of this and nothing else. While I'm wrangling his tongue around in my mouth, squeezing the backs of his thighs, my drunk brain is half aware he's just playing me. That all he cares about is winning, and all I'm doing with this is letting him. But at the same time, I feel like maybe I don't care. Maybe this whole time I've wanted to be played, wanted to give up. Because it's oblivion in here. A blank, swirling high even better than when I'm in the—

"What?"

The light from the hall, more than the voice, startles us. We're suspended in it like a mote of dust. Frozen. Caught. I pull my face away from his. My leg is up, gripped in his hand, my pelvis pressed against his. My shirt up to my collarbone.

"I mean, what—" A voice again from the doorway. Grier. I can't see her face—the light is behind her—but I can imagine her expression.

Gavin lets my leg down slowly. Politely pulls down the hem of my top.

"There you are, baby," he says, like she doesn't know what she just saw, drunk as she may be.

"I just—" There's the shadow of her head, shaking, and then more light blares on, this time shining down on us, on the stupid IKEA desks. The dust bunnies under the chairs. In slow motion, her finger comes up, pointing. I can feel how puffy my lips are, can feel the scrape marks Gavin's dark stubble has left on my face, how stark it must look in this stupid cheap light. I feel the shameful wet pulsing in my pants.

"You," she says, cold. I'm not sure if she means me or Gavin. It's all she says, and then she's gone. The light glares down on us, and everything is deadly silent—even the music from the party seems to have disappeared. I see the rake marks my fingernails have left on his arms, imagine the bare hangers in the closet clanking together in her wake as she storms away.

"Well," Gavin says, clearing the silence and the fog in my head. I look at him: just some college jock, too good-looking for his own good, hiding his dick with his hands.

"Yeah," I say, sinking down to the floor.

31

EVENTUALLY GAVIN DRIVES ME HOME.

First, though, there's the fit with Grier—a call for a cab, fumbling over the address, her angry, waiting in the driveway for an hour and a half before it pulls in, the Ethiopian guy behind the wheel both pissed and apologetic. During the whole wait Gavin tries to get her to let him drive her home, but she just screams curses every time he comes near her. For a while people from the party become a part of it, checking how she is, telling him to leave her alone. Some girl brings her a cup of water. Grier works herself up higher and higher. At one point Gavin gets close enough for her to land a few punches on his chest. I sit down in the grass. The cab comes. She's still crying, and it seems like she's forgotten me, until she turns, tendons in her neck straining, eyes raccoon wild, and shrieks, "I shared everything with you!" She's drunk, but we can still feel her anger pouring out with the car's exhaust as it drives her away.

"Did you at least give her some cash?" I finally say to him, watching the space of black where the taillights have disappeared.

"You okay?" is all he wants to know.

I do a mental check, scanning myself with my interior eyeballs. Nothing broken. Everything intact. But his kindness right now is not anything I can stand.

"Get ready for a bunch of angry texts coming your way," he says. "I'm sure my phone's already full."

A surge of hatred swells in me. Stupid Grier. Thinking he would amount to more than exactly this. Making me prove it to her. And then making such a big deal of it when it happened just the way I knew it would.

"Take me home," I say. "I'm done."

We're both stone-cold sober now.

"Okay," he agrees. And goes to get his keys.

All the outside lights are on at the house when Gavin stops in my driveway. Mom and Louis are going to wonder, again, why I'm not at Grier's. There's going to be more I'm going to have to explain.

"Are you going to—?" he starts.

"Shut up." My fists are clenched against my hard thighs. Everything is hard.

He touches my elbow. "I'm not sorry."

I look at him.

I'm not sorry either. I'm beyond sorry, into nothing. I feel nothing right now.

"I'll see you Monday at practice."

And I get out of the car.

32

I SLEEP UNTIL MOM COMES TO GET ME FOR BREAKFAST AT TEN.
It still isn't enough. I don't know what time it was when I crawled
into bed last night, and if I dreamed at all, I have no idea now
what about, but I'm still tired. Or hung over. Or both.

"You okay, honey?" Mom says, raising her fingers to her
own chin in a question.

I reach up, feel the scrape marks left by Gavin and his swar-
thy stubble.

"Yeah, I'm fine."

"You and Grier have some kind of a fight?"

I frown at her, not sure how she could possibly know this.

"I just mean, usually you're over at her place. And last weekend. . . . " She studies my face, waiting.

"She's got a new boyfriend" is all I say.

"Well." She nods. "I know how that can change things, certainly. Good thing you have Charlie then." She pats my knee but takes her hand away when my face twists.

"We're glad you'll have breakfast with us," she goes on. "Louis's got bacon and eggs downstairs. And yesterday I made those kitchen-sink muffins you like. You know, for this week. I figured a few extra nutrients wouldn't do you any harm."

Kitchen-sink muffins have got about eighteen ingredients, including wheat germ, oats, shredded carrot, blueberries, and applesauce. We found the recipe when I joined Van's team, and Mom got a rare burst of enthusiasm about my routine. They're good for breakfast before school. They freeze easily. They allow her to pretend she actually cares.

"Thanks, Mom. I'll be down in a minute."

I follow her out my door and down the hall where I duck into the bathroom to check myself in the mirror. It isn't bad, but it isn't good, either. I look like a kid who fell on her roller skates and scraped her chin on the sidewalk. Maybe not that bad. But there's also a pretty impressive hickey just under my collarbone, and a yellow spot below my shoulder where I think Gavin's thumb pressed in.

"Way to be subtle," I say to myself in the mirror.

I put on a baggy T-shirt that covers the hickey and most of my arms. I cannot think about it right now. I need to eat first.

But it's not easy. Louis is on me the second I reach the kitchen. "You and Charlie have a good time at the party last night? Getting pretty serious?" He gives Mom what I guess is supposed to be a privately amused smile.

"You know, we like Charlie so much," Mom says. "We really should have him and his family over for dinner. That would be nice, wouldn't it?"

I don't correct them about Charlie not being at the party, and I don't say anything about dinner, either. Or him, for that matter. It's all just a reminder of what I didn't want—all this involvement, all these people and their feelings. Dragging you down while you're fighting to keep your head above-water. Louis drops a plate in front of me, and I tuck in, trying to listen to only my body right now. Though the thought of that makes me laugh—because that's what I thought I was doing last night, too.

After breakfast I take two aspirin and lie on the couch, watching a movie and dozing a little, but I still feel like ass when it's time to go over to the cemetery. Tired, yes, but also like my body's one of those dried-up vanilla beans with the juicy seeds all scraped out too hard. Nothing but splintery husk on the inside.

Changing clothes upstairs, I avoid my phone on the dresser. I still haven't looked at it after Grier left last night. Part of me wants to chuck it into the pool at this point, because God knows what I'll find when I finally turn it on. Scathing shit from Grier, obviously. It'll be impressive to say the least. And then there's Gavin, too. Last night in the car he said he wasn't sorry. What dumb shit is he going to try and say now? That we'll be boyfriend and girlfriend? Or he can't wait for next time? What am I going to say to Charlie, too, if he wants to hang out this afternoon? I can't put him off again, not unless I want a confrontation. But I also can't face him. Not like this. I wanted him last night, right before . . . But now I feel like it'd be much easier to break up with him than dodge him again this afternoon.

All of it makes me feel worse than I did lying on the couch. On top of that, it's turned sticky and hot when we get out of the car, and I'm sweating before we even walk up the little hill to dad's graveside. Luckily, Granny P paid some ungodly amount of money to the cemetery so we could get a little dogwood tree planted at the base of Dad's grave, but it's still not quite big enough to provide a lot of shade. Standing there, head throbbing, I watch Mom place the lilies she brought—real ones this time—and all I can think about is how quickly they'll wilt and rot. Next week they'll probably be nothing but black goo, just like Dad is now. Nothing.

It's how I feel too: black and gooey, out in the heat. After everything from the last two days, even my ever-cement back muscles want to slip off my bones, slide down around my ankles and into the ground. I watch Mom dust off bits of dry leaves and grass from Dad's stone, Louis standing there with his hands crossed in front of him, sweat beading on his forehead and upper lip, watching her. Letting her do it herself. Being fucking reverent.

Maybe it's because I'm burnt to a crisp inside, but suddenly a deep wash of frustration and sadness falls over me. Here I am, stuck with a sweaty, paunchy stepdad who means well but will never cut it, and a mediocre mom who tries to cover her gross inadequacies with her stupid lilies, her muffins, and her soft, questioning voice. Our main family together time, every week, involves staring at a stone-slab hole filled with a titanium box, inside of which is a scorched, half-crushed mummy who used to be my strong, brave, funny, encouraging, badass father who could lift a car off the ground with his bare hands and who rescued people for a living. So now what?

My eyes prickle and my heartbeat speeds up. I can't even take breath one.

On the ride home, I keep my head back and my eyes closed behind my sunglasses so I don't see what Mom means when she says, "Why, look, honey," as we pull up to the house. I don't care. I just want to get away from them and back in my bed.

But it's Charlie.

On our front step.

And I can tell he's been crying.

Shit.

While Mom and Louis give him their hugs and their back-slaps, I tell myself as many lies as I can about why he might be here. Maybe his sister choked on something at breakfast. Or Maria and Ethan broke up. Possibly it's something about *his* father.

But when he finally turns so I can see his face, I know exactly why he's here.

"Is it true?" he demands as soon as Mom and Louis are inside.

"Charlie—" I start, not sure how to finish.

"See, that's where you were supposed to say, 'Is what true?' or, at least, 'No.'"

I look at him. I wasn't ready for any of this yet. And how the hell does he know?

After too long of a pause, I start, "Charlie, I don't know what else to—"

"Yeah." He holds up his hand and laughs meanly. His face is so bitter. "You do. You know exactly. I can see it all over your face, and not just because of your chin. Which—awesome, by the way."

My hand goes up too late. "It isn't—"

But he's obviously been thinking all this over, sitting there on the step.

"Do you really think I'm that stupid?" His throat works up and down like he's going to spit. "I told myself—I don't even know what. Lies. Fantasies. Useless hopes. I mean, I knew you were just dicking around with me. I knew it. But you kept coming over. Kept wanting me so bad. Every day. All the time. You could've dropped me at any point in all this, and I would've totally understood. I expected it, and probably so did everyone else. I mean, why would you be into someone like me, huh? Someone who can't keep up with you in more than one way? It doesn't make sense. But then, sometimes . . . the way you would look at me . . . even when I knew you needed things to stay cool . . . which was fine, but I'd think . . ." For a quick second I see how much I've hurt him, and I want to reach out, stop him, but then this anger moves in again. "Polo, god damn it, you hung out with my friends."

He's been pacing all around the yard, moving in circles, but now he's completely still, his hands in loose fists at his sides.

"I know." My throat is dry, and my whole body is heavy. "I'm sorry, Charlie—"

But moving even slightly in his direction makes his teeth clench harder, which is when I know there's nothing I can say, even if I could think of the right thing.

He clears his throat. "So, when Grier texts me last night, and then calls me, I think it's just you guys goofing around on her phone like that time before. Whatever—she's just some girl you hang out with, who I barely know. But when I listen to the message this morning, she's crying and telling me she has to be honest with me. When I text back, she's ready with all this shit. Shit about you and some Gavin guy in your club. I don't really believe her, I mean, I still don't actually want to believe her, but now I see your face, and I . . ."

All the anger's drained out of him. But mine is just starting to boil. Grier.

"Should I even try and explain?" I say, meaner than I intend, just at the thought of her and what she's done. My eyes are sticky and my muscles are goo and everything feels like shit, and in steps fucking Grier, making it worse. Fucking, fucking, goddamned Grier.

"I don't really think there's a point, Polo. I mean, I knew you didn't want this, with me. I shouldn't be surprised. It's just that being with you felt better than any stupid shit at the pool I've ever won."

It shocks me, how well I understand at that moment. It pulls my thoughts away from Grier and back to him. Which isn't any better, because of how sad he is.

He clears his throat and straightens up. "I know I've always been a loser to you. So thanks for driving that point home. I mean, I really have to thank you for telling me something I didn't already know."

I should say something right now to stop him, but for some reason I can't.

"You know, I will never be able to stop picturing you and . . .

whoever that guy is." His voice is shaking again. Partly mad, partly more than that. "So from now on, you just imagine me, having to go now and explain to my mom, to all of my friends, that we're broken up. And then you picture me having to answer when they ask me why."

I can't look at him. Only his flip-flops on the grass, the driveway, the sidewalk, tell me he's gone. When I can't hear him anymore, I finally look up. He's moving fast, but he's still close enough for me to see him wipe a fist across his eyes. I want to be sad for him—for myself maybe—and briefly that thing he said about us being together feeling better than the pool echoes in me, but as he disappears around the corner, the sludginess I've felt all day starts to harden. As I sit there, watching after the space where Charlie isn't any longer, the shards begin to prick behind my eyes, and my hands squeeze into fists. Rage whipping up inside me. I can see Grier being mad about Gavin, but she had no right to involve Charlie.

Before, I just wanted to show her how dumb she was being.

Now, I want to make her pay.

33

WAKE.

Pee.

Pajamas off—pull on whatever's handiest. This time the cut-offs and hoodie at the top of the pile of clean laundry I brought up last night but was too pissed to put away.

Make bed, pound pillow.

Downstairs, Louis is sipping his coffee. There's a banana and two peeled hard-boiled eggs on the counter for me, plus two of Mom's muffins. Important week this week. Have to be ready.

I pull my ball cap down over my eyes, grab my bag, and follow Louis to the car.

When we head out of the neighborhood, passing Charlie's house, Louis says, "Hey, is everything okay with you and—?"

"Don't want to talk about it." I wave my hand at a red Mazda coming the other way. "Substitute teacher on her way over to Seymour. From the looks of it, she's going to be late."

I spent some time last night fuming, trying to think of what I could do to get back at Grier, but everything I came up with just felt pathetic. Being upset about Charlie, or making her think I am, will only please her. I can't have her feeling she has anything over me. Not anything at all.

So I go through the motions of school. At lunch I sit as far away from the salad bar as I can, though I don't see Charlie or his friends. They probably took him off campus for a cheer-up-she's-a-cooze burger or something.

I didn't like them anyway.

Seeing Kate sitting in Enviro pulls me out of my black cloud, though, because in all this—god damn it—I forgot about those other two annotations due today for Woodham.

Kate sees me hesitate at the door, and a weird expression crosses her face. It's clear she's been watching for me to come in, but now she turns in her desk and faces forward. She can tell I haven't done them. Well, Kate, don't act surprised.

I peek around the lab stations to see if Chu's at her desk yet—no. Which means I can sneak out, go to Coach Trumbull's office, tell her . . . well, I'll think of something on the way there.

I may also still have an old pass in my bag. I can sign it, go to the library, and try to write something for Woodham there, fast.

Kate's looking at me again. I press my finger to my lips and tiptoe back out of the room. She rolls her eyes, crosses her arms, and stares at the board again. Whatever. I don't care what she thinks. I have to get these freaking things done. I speed walk down the hall, panicking at the thought that I may not even have brought the asshole books with me to school today.

I barely squeak into Woodham's class before the late bell, clutching my lame attempts at the annotations, which are really just me rewording the flap jacket copy (the books were still in my bag, untouched from last week) and adding some limp sentences about how similar Booth's plot seems to a lot of the current "acts of terror" we've had in the last few years. They should be typed, especially since even I can hardly read my hurried handwriting, but there was no way. I guess an F is better than a zero, though Kate's scowl when I walk in makes me feel like I shouldn't have bothered.

"Thanks for covering for me in Enviro," I murmur anyway, as Woodham takes roll. She doesn't even turn around.

What the hell ever, Kate. I don't need your disapproval on top of everything else.

During class, Woodham leads a discussion on the articles we were supposed to read this weekend, which of course I didn't do. Regular homework on top of annotations feels particularly evil if you ask me, but I have to keep my head up and pay attention, because if Woodham calls on you during discussion and you don't try to answer semi-intelligently, he docks participation points. The effort of concentrating on what everyone's saying, plus keeping my face from revealing how lost I am, makes me feel bleary-eyed and cotton-brained by the end of it. It was dumb of me to take this course in the first place, but especially to have it at the end of the day, when I need my energy for practice. I can't do this. I hate Woodham and his class, and the paper is going to be impossible. By the time he's wrapping up, the edges of my vision are crackling, and my hands have gone clammy. I can't have this. Something needs to be done.

Kate nearly leaps out of her chair when the bell rings, which causes a wild solution to rise up in me. Kate is the answer. I haul myself out of my own desk and chase her down the hall. She started all this, after all. Like she said, she owes me.

Standing up so fast gives me a head rush though, and the harsh light makes me blink way too many times. When I call out to her my voice feels rusty, which throws me off. Something's not right. When she turns, it seems like even the animals on her binder are glowering at me, which strikes me as wildly funny. Which is definitely strange.

"You didn't do the annotations did you?" she says. "That's why you skipped Enviro. Why I had to cover for you."

A giggle I can't stop comes out of my mouth. "Sorry." I try to take in a breath. "It was an intense weekend."

"Yeah, well, there's homework tonight, but I didn't write it down for you. You'll have to check the class discussion board on your own."

I'm blinking furiously, trying to keep her still in my vision.

"I'm not really worried about homework right now." I widen my eyes, try to stretch the laugh out of my face. Now my creaky voice is hard, bright, fast. "I've been thinking about Woodham's paper, and about my swim schedule the next couple of weeks. I know you have a lot on your plate, but this whole thing is overwhelming, and I was wondering if you would, you know, be willing to help me out. I mean, more than you've been doing."

She narrows her eyes but doesn't say anything. Something about the way she's acting, how cold she's being, makes me even more hysterical.

"I'd pay you, of course," I gush. "I don't know how much people usually charge for this kind of thing, but I'd be willing to—"

She glances over my shoulder, so I turn: There are two teachers down the hall coming toward us, but they're far enough away that I don't think they heard. When I look back at Kate, her face is blotchy and her eyes look wetter than normal.

"So, I mean, can you? Write it for me?"

"You are such an asshole," she says, low and quiet. Then she turns and starts walking away. The panic grabs me, sharpening everything again. Wilder.

"Kate, listen," I holler, scrambling for what to say. "You're so good at this, and I'm just asking you—"

She wheels around. "The answer is no. And don't ask me anything, about anything, ever again, okay? Just leave me alone. Forever."

Her gross overreaction pisses me off even more. She doesn't have to act like it's such a big deal. People do it all the time. And I bet she could use the money.

"Be a bitch about it, why don't you?" I yell down the hall. That she doesn't even turn around fills me with inexplicable fury. "No wonder you love those sheep!" Anger is swimming up my throat, choking me. "Since you have so much in goddamn common."

34

THE WHOLE MESS WITH KATE, AND HOW UNSTABLE I FEEL, HAS made me forget about anything but drills at practice, until I come in from the locker room and my eyes connect with Gavin's. For a second I feel his mouth all over my neck, his hands all over everywhere else, and I almost turn back around. But my body knows what to do; I blink once, twice, and pull back my shoulders. Looking at him again, I realize he's not angry but tense, not to mention alone, on the bleachers, earbuds in, jaw tight, glaring at Grier, who's surrounded by most of the team. So it's not him I have to worry about. As soon as I walk by, everyone else drops silent. Their you-are-such-a-bitch glares feel like little needles tingling over my neck and into my teeth. Three steps, four, past them all, and I realize I'm breathing shallow and my hands are shaking. I don't know what she's told them, but even Megan, who hates Grier, makes a disgusted sound like I just smoked five cigarettes and then licked the ashtray in front of her. I squat down by the water, blinking, and lift a handful to my face. I breathe slow, trying to calm myself. I don't care about them. Them or Grier, or Charlie, or Kate, or anything else. I care about swimming, and that is all I care about. I tell myself this, standing up. I tense all the muscles in my body, squeezing hard for a count of forty. When I let go, though, I still don't relax.

I wheel my arms around in my sockets, try to force myself to loosen. When Van comes out of his office, everyone straightens up, darting eyes at Grier and taking cues from her. She holds her chin up high, aiming it at me like some kind of amazon spear. I don't meet her eyes or Gavin's, either. Van claps and tells us to get into the water. I take the lane on the farthest right side and watch as everyone else triples and quadruples up in the other lanes, just to not have to swim with me. I grit my teeth and press my goggles into place.

So that we're rested and running on full power for Saturday, this is a taper week, which is a good thing, because I'm swimming like shit. I'm weird and sluggish already, but on top of that, every time I break surface it's like I can hear Grier slapping the water way down at the end of the pool, can feel Gavin trying to send me mental *I'm not sorrys* and *We should talk about this*es in submarine sonar, and can feel and smell and hear the anger of the rest of the team uncurling out at me through the water.

When I struggle back from my last 50 free, Van's there at the end of my lane.

"Don't push it," he says when I look up at him. "Take it slow. Breathe."

I nod, because I'm already breathing too hard to say anything else.

He hands me a kickboard. "Two hundred, steady kick. Slow as you can go."

I take the board from him and nod, feeling relieved, embarrassed, and pissed off at the same time.

When practice is over, Grier sidles immediately up with Kelly, Megan, Siena, and Phoebe—like they're all best girlfriends and always have been. Like she hasn't said scathing things about them to me for over a year. The guys have kept their distance from both me and Gavin, so when it's time for the locker rooms, I move behind them slow, not wanting to be near them but needing to get out of my suit and into dry clothes so I can go home and go to bed. I'm fumbling, being obvious, worried I might trip and fall into them, when Van takes my shoulder and turns me around.

"Anything I need to know about?" he asks, his voice quiet but serious.

I blink, my vision still fuzzy. "No."

His eyebrow arches up, high.

His doubt, his accusation, and his palpable disappointment, plus everything else today, brings up tears again. That I'm being so pussy makes it even worse.

"Just a dumb argument," I say, fighting the ball in my throat.

Van's eyes go to the door of the guys' locker room. "I see."

I swipe at my eyes. "She's overreacting. It'll be fine tomorrow."

"If it's something I should be involved in, here's a chance to let me know, right now. Otherwise, I may have to ask her."

I glance at the pool, and a hallucinatory layer appears over the water through my angry, wet vision: the whole team crowded in their lanes, and me, alone, in my own.

"I can handle it," I tell him, trying to breathe. "I mean—I promise I will."

35

WHEN I FINALLY MAKE IT HOME, I GO STRAIGHT TO MY ROOM and shut the door. Since she's not only involving Charlie but now the whole team, too, I may as well see every horrid thing Grier's slung at me over the weekend so I know what I'm up against. So I know how to fight. I press the on button, and once everything's done blinking and singing, I've got eighteen messages.

The most recent ones aren't from Grier, though; they're from Kate. For some reason, just the sight of her name makes the confusing, frustrating tears I just fought down at the pool spring up again, and it gets worse as I go through what she sent.

Friday night: nothing happened like what you drew in class, but i have finally seen the view from second base!!

Saturday afternoon: how is the reading coming?

And then: if you don't have practice tomorrow, do you want to get together?

Sunday: hey, good luck with the last annos. hope you did okay on the first. connor has been texting me all weekend! i think he may even come over after school monday. (!!!!!!)

And, today, after I asked her to write my paper for me: i thought we were friends, but i guess not. i won't tell w what you asked me to do, but you can stop lying to my face every day now. in fact, i don't want you to say anything to me again, not even that you're sorry. thanks.

"God damn it."

I wipe my eyes hard with the back of my hand, swallowing, swallowing, but still unable to keep a sob from coming out. I'm not sad, really—it's just that I can't stop myself from all this crying. It's like the tears and me are unconnected, even though I am upset. Kate thought I had ignored her, and that's why she was so bent out of shape today. But I hadn't, and she didn't even let me explain, and now she won't help me and this isn't at all my fault. I almost text back that I just now got her messages, but then I realize I wouldn't have ignored Kate at all before. If it hadn't been for fucking Grier.

So I go to Grier's messages next, which is what I meant to do in the first place. The trash-talk that pours out of them immediately dries my eyes and clears my vision: such a cunt.

come get your stupid shit outta my hous. how cd you do this 2
me?????????? u have to have everything don't you fucking bitch
and on and on. I scroll and scroll, the tears replaced by dry
anger. I keep scrolling past her hateful messages from the weekend to the exclamation points and excited questions she'd sent
me before the party on Saturday night. Down, farther, through
her you are the best and thx so much messages, plus the needy,
whiny ones about how Gavin's been ignoring her. Far under
those—and I really, truly hate her now—I find the asshole picture of her and Gavin, bragging to me from the beginning about
how he chose her, not me.

I stare at the tiny photo on my phone, realizing, for the first
time, this is just one of five. The first one—the only one you can
see unless you click on it to show the rest—is Gavin's face in her
chest, taken from above so mostly you see her melony cleavage
and the top of his head. The next one is closeup: their arcing
jaws, smiling lips, and two tongues flicking together. The other
three are of Gavin's sculpted chest, her hand squeezing various
places.

Without giving it another thought, I send the pictures to
myself and open up my laptop. I pull up my e-mail, download
the photos, and at the same time pop open new windows and
browse for her pages. Grier's been on my computer plenty, and
I know she's done that dumb and lazy thing where she just auto-
matically saves the passwords. Within seconds I'm logged in as

her, and I've got the meanest grin on my face. So the whole team thinks I'm a scag? Watch this.

I upload the photos, adding SHE'LL NEVER TAKE HIM AWAY FROM ME captions, and IN YOUR FACE, BITCH. They're stupid, but whatever—Grier is stupid. And in my head it makes sense. Though you can't see her face in any of them, the giant ruby cocktail ring she got when her aunt died (and which she wears on her middle finger so that she can "Flick people off with royalty") is right there in the shot of Gavin's chest. I love how the flash catches it as she's pinching his nipple, her pinky finger held out like she's sipping tea. For a second, just to make sure everyone knows they're really of her, I consider tagging Gavin, and myself, even, but then I think crazily that if I do, then maybe Charlie will somehow see them, even though he's barely online, and why would he care about photos of Grier, anyway?

So I don't. Instead I post without hesitation across the board. And then I sit there and smile as the comments start coming in.

36

AS MUCH AS I'M DESPERATE FOR SLEEP, THERE ARE BAD dreams that night. The worst one's about being held inside some giant warehouse where there are a lot of Chinese kids making video-game parts. I'm walking around observing them under a wolf mask. Maria's dad is up on the catwalk, looking down at all of us. And I know he's going to jump. It jerks me so hard out of sleep that it takes what feels like a whole minute for my heart to calm down. I spend an hour on the couch by the TV, but it doesn't work, and I finally go back to my bed, where I guess I do sleep for a couple of hours. When the alarm goes off though, I want to kill it.

But I'm also getting sick of all this. I march down to the bathroom, turn on the cold water, and splash several handfuls over my face. I don't grab a towel. I just lean forward over the sink, glaring at myself in the mirror and watching the droplets slide down, following the snaky lines of my wet hair around the edge of my forehead. I seize my rib cage in the claws of my two hands and squeeze, hard, feeling the edges of my bones roll under my thumbs. When I can't take a normal inhale, I let go.

"It's handled for now," I say into the mirror. "So get over yourself. Get over yourself right this minute."

For the first time ever, I down a Dr Pepper right before school. I slug another one at lunch, and then after Enviro, where I sat on the total opposite side of the room from Kate. As soon as that class ends, so that there isn't any confusion about my obeying her wishes to never speak to her again, I beeline past her and across the building down to the vending machines, where I stand there, one hand still on the button, slamming down a Coke Zero. I know it's only false strength, and probably I'll still be late to Conflicts, but yesterday was bullshit and if this works, so be it.

When I pause in my glugging for a much-needed burp, though, I see Nora and Maria walk past. At first I think they're just going to pretend I don't exist, but then Maria tugs on Nora's elbow and turns around.

I finish my soda and make off for the recycling bin, but she's quickly beside me.

"You really broke his heart," Maria says, her pretty brown eyes glaring.

I blink, wide, chemicals pulsing in me. All the tiredness and confusion are gone; I feel like I could break her over my knee.

"And you think I need this news flash why?"

It makes her back down half a notch. She sees me seeing it, and I smile.

"It's just that . . ." she tries again, switching from bad cop to good cop right in front of me. "He's not the kind of guy who dates around. You're the first since Sarah."

"I know it."

It's like she wants tears from me or something. But the ones from yesterday were already too much. I stare at her, bored, saving my energy for more important things.

"It must be nice for you up there on your high horse," she finally says, exasperated. "I just hope it doesn't trample you when one day you fall off."

I laugh as she heads, flustered, back to Nora. It's not that I'm really laughing at her. It's just that she has no idea how wrong she is: I'm not on this horse; I've fucking fused myself to it. I couldn't fall off if I wanted to.

The outrage at Nora and Maria helps fuel me through Conflicts. I make it through Kate ducking her head down the moment I come in, make it through her stinky-ass feet and the cold silence rolling off her back. At the end of the day, I wait for her to leave, faking a question for Woodham, and then I trudge, alone, out to Louis and the car. We drive to practice. He doesn't ask me anything.

It's fine.

Still, when we get there, everything looks edgy and bright under the fluorescent lights at the pool, like on a high-def TV, and my insides feel lined with aluminum tendrils, but at least I don't feel like my body's just walking around with a soggy, weepy brain inside anymore. I'm still getting the silent treatment from everyone in the club, but since Grier, interesting enough, isn't at practice, the hate beams are a little more diffused. At least Dylan gets in the same lane as me today. Gavin's trying to catch my eye too, wants to say something, I guess, since I've ignored all his texts since Saturday, but I keep my eyes on the water. On the clock. On Van's face. I can't mess with him or anyone else.

There are only three more easy practices after this one until qualifiers.

And nothing else matters.

I do check Grier's pages from my own accounts when I get home, just out of curiosity. Every single photo I posted yesterday has been deleted, and the comments have disappeared with them. Which means she saw them and freaked out.

Which is very, very good.

37

WEDNESDAY IS THE SAME THING, INCLUDING THE CAFFEINE, because even though I feel better, I'm still not sleeping right. Last night it wasn't dreams, but instead me lying there worrying about what I'd do if I had them again, and then what if I couldn't fall back asleep. That went on until about one in the morning. And then I had to be up at six thirty.

The sodas work their magic though, and the day itself is unremarkable, except that Kate is still ignoring me, and also that Van seems really distracted at practice. He spends a third of the time pacing around the end of the pool on his phone, and twice he snaps at Dylan for goofing around. Grier's still gone, and when Phoebe asks about it at pep talk, all Van says in his terse voice is that Grier's not feeling well and needs to really rest up for Saturday. The way Phoebe bites her lip and looks at Kelly, I can tell she's thinking what everyone's thinking, which is that with zero practice this week, Grier probably shouldn't even show up to the meet.

Whether it's glee over Grier, or caffeine or what, I'm far better today than the last two days, even though we're still supposed to go slow. I don't know what my problem was Monday, but that's obviously all over. I'm back on my game.

So when I see Gavin talking to Louis when I come out of the locker room, I'm more amused than anything else.

"You didn't tell me Louis was a track man," Gavin says right away, clapping my stepdad on the shoulder like they're old pals. "Hurdles aren't for sissies."

I look at him, then Louis, trying to hide my confusion. Not about the two of them talking, but about the two of them talking about something I've never heard of.

"Ah, it was a long time ago," Louis says, rubbing his knee, the one he wears a brace on sometimes doing yard work, or when he and Mom go ride bikes. The look he gives Gavin makes it clear he doesn't want him to say anything more, but I already get it. Suddenly the whole supersupportive stepdad routine makes a lot more sense.

"So—what?" I ask, deflecting the topic, and my own minor shock. "You guys just standing around, trading war stories?"

"A little bit like that," Gavin says jovially. "But really, I was waiting for you. Thought we could maybe go catch a bite. Talk more about . . . Auburn. I could give you some tips for Saturday."

I glance over at Louis. The week before a major meet, Mom makes sure to have these elaborate dinners at home to help me calorie-load. It's kind of a big deal. At least for her. Besides, I know Gavin doesn't really intend to talk about college, and there isn't anything else to say about the rest. It happened, and it's done. I don't give a shit about whatever's going on with Grier or him. I'm finished with letting him screw with me. I have to stay focused for the rest of the week.

"Karen's got something planned tonight," Louis apologizes.

"Oh. Well—a milk shake or something?" Gavin's apparently determined. "It won't take long. I just had some pointers I wanted to—"

"Why don't you join us for dinner?" I say to shut him up, get him to go away.

The panicked look he gives me is priceless. "Oh, I wouldn't want to impose."

I hook my elbow in his, realizing this will be a great way to torture him.

"Come on. You're such a stiff. We can talk while Mom and Louis make dinner. You probably could use a home-cooked meal anyway, right? I mean, your times are still important on Saturday too. College bracket still counts, after all."

I blink up at him, giddy at my own unexpected brilliance. He wants to "talk" about what happened with Grier? Fine. But we will do it on my terms.

"Sure, yeah," Louis says, scratching his head and reaching for his phone. "Let me double-check."

"What the hell are you doing?" Gavin whispers fierce while Louis steps away. "I only wanted to talk."

"So we're going to talk."

"This isn't what I meant."

"So what did you mean? That you were going to drag me off on your own and get me half naked again? Hm? Then, since it seems like that's your pattern, go back to Grier and start all over? That what you had in mind? Not enough of it on Saturday?" My voice is thickly sweet but bitter-bright. I am dizzy with power.

"That isn't what happened, and you know it. Jesus. You're as crazy as she is."

That part makes me curious, but before I can say anything back, Louis tucks his phone back into his pocket. "All set," he says, coming toward us with a smile. "And Karen's looking forward."

38

OF COURSE GAVIN ALREADY KNOWS WHERE MY HOUSE IS, BUT it's still delicious watching Louis signal way too early for the turns, constantly checking his rearview, making sure not to lose Gavin following behind us. He pumps me for all the information I have, which, in terms of what I can tell my stepdad, isn't much, and then tries to act all in the know when he finally introduces Gavin to Mom. They grill him about Auburn, his high school team, his plans for the future, and it's funny for a while to watch Gavin squirm, but I finally pull him off to the den where he can "help me out as much as possible." I worry at first that Mom might ask me later if Gavin's why I'm not hanging out with Charlie anymore—the look on her face when she sees how good-looking he is means it crosses her mind—but after a few minutes in the kitchen, Gavin all stiff and formal, it's clear she and Louis think he's some impressive coach for me, which makes the whole thing even funnier. I didn't even mean to play it this way, and still I'm winning.

"I shouldn't be here," he grumbles when we're finally alone, each tucked into our corner of Louis's giant L-shaped couch.

"Oh, come on. It's just dinner. And Louis loves you."

"Yeah, thanks for that. You girls are nuts."

I wiggle my eyebrows at him. "I thought you wanted us to be into those."

"It's not like that, Jesus. Will you calm down? It's what I wanted to talk about if you would just listen. I don't know what Grier's said to you, but I'm sure you saw what she did."

I hold my face still, but it's hard not to smile.

"That shit she posted online? That was all her. I didn't even want to take those pictures."

I scoff to hide my delight. "Don't pretend you're sorry. Besides, nobody knows for sure it's you, so why do you care? And why do you think that I would?"

"I don't know." He sighs. "Everything was just so fucked up on Saturday, and you won't answer my texts or even look at me in practice, so I wanted to make sure."

Victory swirls over me, making me dizzy.

"You wanted to make sure of what, exactly?"

He rakes his hand over the top of his head. "Make sure you knew I was done with her. That girl is a disaster. It isn't like that with you. I mean, the way it was with me and her. I wasn't—"

I cross my arms, pretending to be mad. "So, what? I'm not hot enough for you?"

The weak, exasperated look on his face is so satisfying, I almost exclaim aloud.

"That's not what I mean," he whispers, glancing at the den's entryway, though the kitchen's down the hall, and Mom and Louis have some Internet radio program going on anyway, so it's not like they could hear.

I scoot closer to him, put my hand up high on his hard thigh. "What exactly do you mean then, hm?"

I can see he thinks he should push me away, but he doesn't.

"I mean, you're different. You aren't like half the girls I know at school. Sure, you're unbelievably hot, don't get me wrong, but maybe I want to actually know you."

I want to hop up, right there, and do a touchdown dance in the middle of the living room. I wish I had a recorder on so I could play what he just said over and over. Take that, Grier. Take that and that until you die purple.

The sound of Mom's house shoes in the hallway breaks us apart.

"Well, that's all very interesting, and I really appreciate it," I say, leaning back in the couch cushions and away from him.

"I just want you to know, I'm serious," he says, voice all coachy-enthusiastic, but eyes still making a point.

"Sounds like it's going well," Mom says, peering in at us. "And I hope you're hungry."

"Oh, yeah," I say, growl, rubbing my tummy, and flashing a grin. "Totally starved."

Mom's made lemon-roasted chicken and the wild rice salad with dried apricots that I like, plus a spinach salad for extra iron, and there's dessert, of course. She and Louis sit at their ends of the table, which leaves Gavin and I across from each other. Through most of the meal, because it's hilarious, I keep snaking my bare foot under the table and up his leg. For almost three whole minutes my foot's there, heel pressed against the taut fly of his jeans, moving up and down. At one point he reaches under the table and presses my foot even harder against him, which makes me flush. He gives me a glimmering look under those thick eyelashes, and then coughs and half-stands, reaching over to take another chicken leg from Mom and then pushing my foot away with his other hand.

He can push me away, but I know I can still do anything to him.

I can do anything I want.

When dinner's over and Gavin's refused Mom's second attempt to make him a cup of coffee, I walk him out to his car.

"So when am I going to finally get you on my own?" he wants to know. He's draped in the driver's seat but facing me with his knees open. The hungry eyes he had at the dinner table take over. I thought, after his little you're-actually-interesting bit in the den, that he might be turning all pussy on me but apparently not.

"You have to wait until after Saturday. I've got to conserve my energy." I'm facing him with my back against the open car door, but as I say this, I rock my hips forward a little, just to tease him. Just to keep it going.

"That'll be a long wait." He reaches out, grabs the belt loop on my shorts, and pulls me closer. He slips the tips of his fingers down between the waistband and my skin, sending a shiver up my abs. "You aren't going to give me something to hold me over?"

I lock my knees and squeeze my quads tight.

"What? Hand job out here in my driveway? Much as Louis likes you, I don't think he'd go for that."

He makes a low growl and lifts my hand to his lips. I watch as his tongue flicks gently between my fingers and then as he engulfs one of them in his mouth. His eyes stay on mine as the wet tip of his tongue tickles along the bottom of my finger. Against my will, even my elbows swirl with heat.

"Maybe tomorrow," I find myself murmuring.

"Tomorrow?" he asks, still nibbling.

"You can come over. After Mom and Louis are in bed."

I sleep fine that night.

And there aren't any dreams.

39

MAYBE IN RESPONSE TO DINNER WITH GAVIN, OR MAYBE
because of it, but on Thursday morning I'm back to full-on normal. Nothing fazes me, not even that I don't have my flash cards
finished for Spanish. I just make my excuses to Señora Gupta
about the meet this Saturday and how important it is, and say
that I'll have everything by Monday. She smiles her tired smile
and says okay, as long as I do ten extra.

Not even Kate and her steady silence across the room in
Enviro can bother me. Not her tall, solid, uninterested back
in Conflicts, either. Today I don't have to sleep through lunch,
and I don't need any caffeine, either. So bring it, everyone. Just
bring it the fuck on.

· · ·

Practice, though, is a little weirder. Grier's still not there, and enough of the team seems worried about her that they break their vows of silence to ask me if I've heard anything. Like she and the whole rest of them weren't totally cold-shouldering me just a couple of days ago.

"She's fine," I tell them, cool. "She just needs a break. Hard as Van's been driving us toward Saturday, we could all use it, right? Let's make sure we don't make her even more sorry by fucking up ourselves."

It's bullshit, and I could care less about Grier anymore. That it took them only three practices to give up on hating me is the important part. If it were me, I would've held out for much, much longer.

What makes things even stranger though is that Gavin isn't there either. And neither is Linus or Troy. That Van doesn't say anything about it—that he acts like everything is perfectly normal—makes us all shoot questioning looks at one another through pep talk. Something is going on, but Van's not telling. Not even when I ask him point-blank, before we get into the pool, where the three guys are.

"Just adjusting their schedules" is all he says, terse. "Worry about yourself, not them." And then sends me on a 200 free, descending times.

what happened? I text Gavin after practice.

But I don't get anything back.

• • •

I don't get anything back at 9:30, either, when I send: **getting ready for bed. you still coming?** I lay in bed last night picturing how tonight would go: He'd come over, I'd sneak out, and we'd make out a bit in his car down the road. I haven't had any action since that catastrophe on Saturday night, and I won't lie that I miss it, especially now that I can't have Charlie, either. I know it's partly why I haven't been able to sleep. But with Gavin, it'll be even better, because unlike Charlie, I know I can count on Gavin not to want to talk, no matter what he said last night. I can get what I need and then send him away, easy. Even though I felt basically all right today, I still need at least a decent eight hours tonight and another eight tomorrow for sure. Ten would be better. Getting off a bit will definitely do the trick. Tending to myself is all right, but it's not the same. Still, I'm also not dumb. I need to maintain the upper hand. So we'll fool around in his car for a while and then I'll say something about how tired I am, how I need to get to bed. If he protests, I'll promise—and I'll be convincing—to make it up to him after the meet. Fingers crossed behind my back, of course.

But now it's 10:12, 10:26, and there's still not a beep from him, not even after I send three more texts. Stupidly, I even try trolling through Grier's pages for a while just to see if he's been on any of them. But they've both been silent for days. I picture Grier having to go back to those shopping bitches. It makes me wonder for a few seconds how she's doing without anyone to talk to. But then, of course, I realize Gavin's also not showing up anywhere because Grier's disconnected herself from him since Monday, and besides, I don't care about her anymore, after what she did.

Disconnecting from Gavin doesn't sound like a bad idea for me, either, except now it seems as if he's leaving me hanging, and I can't have that. He laid on that cheese about wanting to get to know me, I offered to sneak out for him on a school night, and now he can't even text back? I lie in my bed in the dark with my knees up, balancing my phone between them, waiting. If he had late practice, as Van suggested today, maybe it's taken him this long to finish, eat, get showered, and head over. *Maybe*, I tell myself lamely, *he forgot to charge his phone.* But I know that's beyond pathetic. It makes me wish I could take all those stupid texts back.

It's 11:09. I shouldn't be up, but I am. Part because maybe he's still coming over, part because I'm mad, part because I'm trying to think how I'm going to get him back for standing me up. I get out of bed and pace. Now, instead of being rested and calm tomorrow, that edgy feeling will creep back over me all day, and what if I can't shake it? Being off at practice only screws me up in the head more. So I really need to get some sleep. It's dumb that I haven't been able to for the last several nights. I think about my routine tomorrow, how I'm supposed to float through the day to relax myself before the race Saturday. And look at me right now—pacing around like a crazy animal, working myself up too tight.

A car outside on the street makes me stop and go to the window. I watch the headlights approach slow, and then keep watching as a car that's not Gavin's goes past our house and down the road. My mind jumps around, wondering was he in some accident, wondering did he get in trouble about Grier, then chastising myself for wasting any thought on him at all, when the only person I need to worry about is me.

"You can't worry though, is the thing," I remind myself out loud. Because fixating on a thing—swimming or winning or not crying or some noncommunicative college cockhead—is exactly the way to fuck it all up.

Your mind has to be completely blank. It has to be.

Which makes me pause and turn to the door.

Alcohol is stupid, because it dehydrates you and makes you all groggy. Besides, Mom and Louis don't keep anything around except her cheap gross wine and his beer, which they'd notice was gone. It'd be better if I could somehow get some pot. The next best thing is Mom's Ambien or whatever is down there in her medicine cabinet. She started taking it after Dad's accident and then kept going, thanks to her work and Louis's snoring problem. It'll be tricky, and I'll have to be deadly silent, but I know it will work.

I go to my door and turn the knob slow. Out in the dark

hallway, I pause, listening, but I wouldn't be able to hear anything from their bedroom at the back of the house anyway. I move down the hall, heel to toe like I read somewhere the Indians used to do. At the top of the stairs, I pause again. I don't have to do this. With the right breathing, I could probably fall asleep. Eventually. But then I picture myself on the couch the other night, eyes unable to close. I picture the dreams I can't afford to have.

I lower my foot to the first step. I will be silent, and I will master this.

I can do absolutely anything.

40

LOUIS'S VOICE COMING FROM MY DOORWAY IS THE ONLY THING that wakes me up.

"Brynn? Time to get a move-on, kiddo. You feeling okay?"

"Yeah," I manage to tell him, hauling myself out of a dark tunnel. Once I can register my body, the inside of my mouth feels like snakeskin, and it's like someone's been pressing their heels into my eyeballs all night. I pull them open, looking at my alarm clock in betrayal. But it's beeping away, faithful as ever. "Just gimme a minute."

I pull myself to a sitting position. My whole body feels heavy and soft like a damp down pillow. This is not the way today is supposed to start.

I can't panic though. Today I have to be in control. So as

soon as Louis leaves, I work to remember my visualizations. Day before a huge race, it's important to do things as easily and gently as possible. Though it's clouded and slow, I clear my mind of any clinging thoughts, including the picture of my own hand, popping that pill into my mouth last night. Instead I have to visualize myself floating through the day, like I'm on feathers the whole time. Which maybe won't be so hard, weird as I feel. I picture myself gliding through school, not bumping into anyone or getting stressed or jostled by anything my teachers say, whatever happens in class. I follow myself in my mind to the end of school and then practice, which will be nothing but a few warm-up drills, mostly. Gentle. Easy. After that, I picture me and mom and Louis sitting together at Maggiano's for a huge dinner. Pasta. Meatballs. Maybe shrimp scampi. Then home and some light stretching and into bed. Drinking nothing but water the whole time and always breathing calm and slow—drifting through the day. Nothing will stress me out. Nothing will shake me.

Not even the fact that it's hard to stand up.

When I get to school, I'm tempted to go straight to the Coke machine again, just to shake off this groggy cloud, but the discipline in me knows I need water instead. Flush this shit out and rehydrate my muscles. Normalize. So between every class, while I'm trying to float, I make sure to stop at every single water fountain I pass and take a sip. By third period it becomes part of the ritual, and at lunchtime I'm only slightly fuzzy. At least my mouth doesn't feel like death. When I get to Enviro, I'm clearheaded enough to register that Kate keeps twitching and scowling at me from across the room, instead of playing the ice queen role she has been all week.

But I can't think about it.

Nothing can faze me.

I think about floating, and that is all.

It's harder when she's sitting in front of me in Conflicts, and I can feel the frustration coming off her in waves. Harder to ignore the way her knee jerks up and down in nervous agitation all through class, but I make myself do it. I don't know what her problem is all of a sudden—why today she's fidgety and pissed, when the whole week it's like I haven't existed—but I can't let it be my problem. While she jiggles and huffs, I close my eyes, picture myself floating in the middle of a great expanse of blue: too deep to hear or see anything. Too deep for anyone to touch.

Even when Woodham reminds us that the first drafts of our papers are due Monday and he reviews the expectations, I pull my breath, gentle and slow, in through my nose and out through my mouth. I visualize myself on the block tomorrow, ready to race. That's what matters right now. It's all that matters. The rest I will figure out how to make happen, because everything else this whole week—my whole life—I have more than figured out on my own, I've aced. I picture bubbles floating, floating through my veins. I pretend I'm gliding smoothly through a vast and empty plane of water. I am a swimmer, and that's all I am.

Practice solidifies this feeling even more. Van has us do some breathing exercises and a little yoga to stretch us out before we even get into the pool. During pep talk he stresses personal victories, and confidence, and trusting ourselves and the work we've done to succeed tomorrow. And, cheesy as it may be, tense as he's been the last couple of days, Van's encouraging, confident voice always centers me.

I don't have to pull or push or do anything through the drills. I'm in the water, and that's all I am. Nothing fazes me. Everything is mastered.

When Mom, Louis, and I get home from our huge Italian feast, it's 8:30, which is plenty of time to prep my stuff for tomorrow, take my pre-meet bath (and supershave), and then have a last bit of protein before bed. While I'm checking my suits for any wear and making sure I have a clean towel, my phone buzzes on my dresser.

Suddenly the calm, easy, floating feeling is gone. It's startling, actually, how fast it leaps away from me, how quickly I'm back on edge. I stare at my phone, not moving. Gavin messing with me. Or apologizing. Or maybe Kate sending me some poison she's been thinking of all week and didn't have the nerve to say to my face. Grier, maybe, trying to fuck with my head before tomorrow. Or maybe even someone else from the team. I shouldn't go to it—I shouldn't even pick the phone up. It's taken a lot of work to hit this even-keeled place, and the way my brain is snapping all around now, apparently it may take more to get it back.

But I can't let anyone get the last word on me. Especially not if it's Gavin. I can't let anyone throw off my control.

When I finally lift the phone, all it says is **good luck tomorrow. Charlie.**

I stare at the message, my heart racing.

thanks I type back, holding my breath, eyes blinking, feeling weird.

I put the phone back down and ignore my own shaking. After that, I calmly walk down the hall, draw the bath, and sink into the bubbly warm water. I soap up my arms and my legs, and shave everything slow. The whole time, I force myself to breathe, put myself in that blue expanse of water where there's nothing but me, floating. Deep, deeper, so, so deep.

I think about floating. That is all I think.

41

EXCEPT I DON'T FLOAT. INSTEAD I LIE THERE IN BED, THINKING of Charlie, and Grier, and Van trying to push us all, and stupid Gavin and his mind games, and how I called Kate a sheep. I think of John Wilkes Booth on the run after shooting the president, and of Maria and her happy family. I think of going downstairs and trying one of Mom's pills again, and then I think of how shitty it made me feel and how that can't happen. I think of my disappointed teachers, of college, and parties, and sex, guys playing guitars, friends I had once, and ones I have never had. I think so much, I press my hands against my eyes, and then I still can't stop thinking. I am not calm. I am not floating. I am nowhere near the water, and I feel like I'm going to drown.

I jerk awake at 6:05, panicking that I've slept through my

alarm again, though it won't start buzzing for another half hour. Relieved, I try to assess how I'm feeling. Tired isn't exactly the word. I've been plenty tired in the last few weeks, and this doesn't feel like that. Perturbed, more like. Wary. Like something's going to jump up on me at any minute. A message from a phone. A backstabbing friend. A memory or an unwanted dream. My own weakness.

"Quit freaking yourself out, pussy," I say into the dark room.

The unflinching sound of my own voice helps me get up and start the routine. Van likes to say you only make this path by walking, and I know the only way I'll win this race today is by doing it. Instead of visualizing myself floating now, it's time to see myself winning, see myself achieving the times I need to bring me to State. No matter what else is lurking in my mind, I shove it away to do my breathing. I do my stretches. I go downstairs, where Louis hands me a plate of egg whites and a glass of grapefruit juice he squeezed himself. I'm doing everything right. I'm doing it all.

When we get to the pool, I smile and nod at everyone. It's a way to fool both yourself and them into thinking you're relaxed. I do it at every meet. It usually works. People nod back, but mainly everyone's got their earbuds in, listening to whatever tunes they need to get themselves pumped. Even mine are in, though it's more for show than anything else. I never need music to get amped for a race. More often, I need it to help calm me down.

Today, though, there's nothing but silence. Nothing but me.

I sit on the bleachers with my teammates, and we watch the parents moving to their seats, greeting one another, many of them wearing jerseys for their different schools or clubs. The other teams come in, all of them blank-faced and not watching us just as much as we are blank-faced and not watching them. Next to me, Shyrah's leg starts jittering up and down. I reach out and touch his arm lightly to make him stop, and he smiles, apologetic. I understand—I'm on edge too. Not about Gavin, since the college bracket isn't until this afternoon and we won't be around to see them swim. Not even about Grier really, because by now it's clear she's not coming and is probably off the team. Instead it's the paranoid feeling I had this morning: the feeling that something's waiting to jump out.

Van comes back from greeting the other coaches, and we circle around him for his final pep talk. He tells us about focus. He reminds us about hard work. He says the things he always says about nothing mattering but swimming well, and that chasing ribbons and medals aren't what we're here for. He says the things that always work, because he's right. But then his voice shifts.

"As I know you've suspected, I found out for sure yesterday afternoon that Grier's decided to take a permanent break from the team."

Phoebe makes a sound of protest, but a look from Kelly

stops her. I feel a few of the others shifting their gazes to me.

"That still shouldn't affect your performance today, and she told me she didn't want it to either. I know there have been some other adjustments this month too, like working out the right schedule with the college trainers, all of which you've handled really well, so I know you'll take this in stride. It's been a boon to me, actually, your dedication, in spite of the challenges you may have felt. So before you get out there, I want to thank you, personally, and say that I'm always proud of you, but right now, this moment, I am especially so."

Something's wrong with his voice. I look up at him, catching the end of his grimace before he straightens out his expression. He clears his throat and goes on.

"I just want you each to know that no matter what, I believe in all your abilities because I've seen what you can do. And I respect and value each of you, not just as swimmers but as people, too."

It's a weird speech. Not that weird, I guess, but Van's wobbliness is. I keep watching him as we put our hands in the center of the circle, say our victory chant, and then throw our hands up in the air and break, but the only thing that seems odd about him now is that he won't make eye contact with me.

There are a few minutes for a last trip to the bathroom, so most of us head that way. I stay in the stall until everyone's left, puzzling over Van, and Grier dropping the team. Not that I care. She's been hating on swimming way before all this, so it isn't much of a surprise, but it's weird knowing I could potentially now never see her again. Weird how sentimental Van's being too. Weird also that since Gavin left my house for dinner, I still haven't heard from him. That Charlie, after what I did, still wanted to send me good thoughts last night.

I let myself out of the stall. Go to the sink and lean into the mirror, close.

"Stop thinking about them," I tell my reflection. "It's time to focus on you. You don't need her. You never did. You are a better swimmer than her and everyone else, and that she can't hack it is only her fault. She wasn't even your real friend before all this, just a fun escape. And Gavin is a dick who you've already bested. You didn't care about Charlie until just over a month ago either, so stop thinking about that stupid message and what it might mean. It means good luck. That's all it means. And you don't need luck. You are the best swimmer here, and you got that way without all of them. On your own. So go out there, and fucking forget it. You go out there, and you swim the way you've built yourself to, and nothing else."

I stand up straight, pulling my shoulders back tight and squeezing hard. I clench my quads, right, left, right, left. I scowl at myself in the mirror, my brows twisted with contempt. I meet my own gaze, unafraid. I am not weak. Look at all this shit I can take.

I wait there until I know I can walk out of the bathroom and leave it all behind.

Everything else can go fuck itself.

42

I HAVE TO SIT THROUGH THREE RACES BEFORE IT'S MY TURN, but watching how everyone else succeeds and fails helps take my mind further off anything but swimming. As they move through the water, I pretend I'm moving with them. By the time I'm walking up to the block, it's almost weird that my suit isn't wet like theirs. I roll my shoulders, loosen my neck. I check where Van's standing: in the middle of the pool to my right, where he gives me a solemn nod and a thumbs-up. The buzzer sounds, and we all step up. On the block, I stare down the lane, picturing myself in the final fifty, the closest girl a whole length in my wake. Another buzzer sounds, and we lean over, fingers to the edge. I am seeing myself winning. I am seeing nothing else.

And then—buzz.

Leap.

Stretch.

Pull.

The water surrounds me. I pull and pull and pull and pull.

Turn, push, breathe, and pull again, the whole time think-ing only one, clear, invigorating thing: Fuck everyone else. Fuck everything but this.

At the second turn, I can see the girl to my left inching closer. Van's waving three fingers in the air at me from the side, which means *Go faster*. So I do. Kicking strong, feet together, rising up, and coming down. Pull. Pull. Pull. Pull. My whole body is doing only this one thing.

Final turn. I can't see anyone anymore, but I'm not wor-ried. All I see is the blood thrashing through my arteries, oxygen pouring into my giant lungs, my whole body working through the water. And then I see my hand touching the wall, and I see the board.

My time. My name in first place. And then bits of darkness creeping at the edges of my vision. I toss my head to make them go away. The girl next to me reaches over the lane divider. As we shake, our hands look like they're detached from us, made of rubber. We're both breathing hard, but I can't get enough air. Somewhere I hear Louis's loud, sharp whistle in the crowd—a sound of pride from far away. I pull myself out of the pool, and the black spots get bigger. I've won, but something's not right.

Van is smiling, clapping me on the back. I look at the board again; my name there in red.

It's the last thing I see before everything goes black.

I wake up. Mom is working my hand in hers and looking at me, scared. Louis is behind her, leaning down and gripping her shoulder. Van's bending over my other side. There's some kind of medic. She puts a mask over my face, and the rush of oxygen makes me light-headed again. I reach to swat it off.

But I can't lift my hand.

They're taking me somewhere. I'm moving. Mom is on the phone. There's something in my arm—some kind of tube.

"Louis is right behind us in the car, honey," Mom says when she sees my eyes are open. I try to nod. She goes back to whoever she's talking to. The medic says something, but I don't hear it.

Dehydration, they tell us, after all the tests and they've assigned me to a room. Extreme exhaustion. They want me to stay here overnight, give me fluids, they say. They want me to sleep, make sure I'm balanced.

It doesn't make sense.

It doesn't make any fucking sense.

I had it all under control.

Louis and Mom sit together by my bed, watching me. They already had their questions answered. By me, by the doctors. *I don't know what happened,* I tell them. That, and I'm fine.

Mom wants to know do I want anything; she's getting some coffee.

"You should just go home," I say. "There isn't anything to do but sit here and watch these fluids drip into my arm." Plus, I don't want her here, or Louis, either, looking at me, wondering what happened, when I don't even know. She tells me I'm crazy if she thinks she's leaving me by myself. I'm too tired to laugh, tell her she already left me a long time ago.

Van comes by, later. He has a card signed by the rest of the team. His face is worried, but he tries to hide it by smiling and telling me I did great. I don't know what to say except thanks, and that I'm sorry. He pats me encouragingly on the foot, and then he, Mom, and Louis go out in the hall and talk for a long time.

There isn't a lot else. At some point in the night I'm aware of a nurse coming in and something getting checked or changed. Mom on a cot next to me. Louis asleep in the chair. I want to fight it, but I can't, the dark sleep pulling me down.

The next day, they bring in breakfast, but I only want to eat the slippery, sweet canned peaches. Mom and Louis have

Chick-fil-A they bought down in the lobby, and the smell makes me sick, but I don't ask them to throw it out. The doctor comes in again, says everything's okay. I can go. There's paperwork that Mom and Louis handle. They insist on wheeling me out, though I tell them, over and over, that I can walk just fine on my own.

43

WHEN WE GET HOME, THERE'S NO MENTION OF GOING TO THE cemetery. I head straight for the couch and stare at the TV, feeling bloated and hazy from all the stuff they pumped into me at the hospital. I still don't know what happened. I won, I made State, and yet I'm lying here feeling like a lame-o. I can't work it out in my head.

Mom and Louis make sure I have what I need, and then they go into their room and shut the door. Eventually there's the sound of the shower starting up. Louis comes in to check on me then disappears again to the back of the house. When Mom comes back, she's in a wrap skirt and what she considers a "cute top," and she's brought out a plate of crackers, plus cream cheese with pepper jelly smeared over it.

"What's going on?" I pull myself up to a sitting position. Seeing her showered makes me realize I should probably take one too.

Before I can even lean forward to get up though, there's a knock at the door, and Louis goes to get it. Van's standing there, holding flowers and wearing pressed khakis, when I've never seen him in anything but shorts, even in winter.

"You guys plan some kind of intervention or something?" I try to make it sound like a joke, but Mom's guilty smile cuts me off mid-laugh.

"Van just wanted to come over and talk with you, honey," she says, blinking at him then Louis. She hustles away quickly to put the flowers in a vase.

"How you feeling?" Van asks, sitting on the other end of the couch.

"Fine." The way he's looking at me, the way Mom and Louis are being, sharpens my defensiveness. "I told you, I don't know what happened. But I guess it didn't matter did it, right? I mean, I won."

Van looks at Louis, who's sitting bolt-straight in the recliner across from me.

"You definitely did," Van says, "though I can say what happened also matters quite a lot. Dehydration and exhaustion are serious things, Brynn. They take time to recover from. We need to make sure it's not going to happen again."

"I did nothing but sleep at the hospital. I'm so full of fluids, my eyeballs are floating."

Van nods, not really listening. "Yes, they got you normalized, but you still need more time." He glances at Mom, who's come back into the room. "It's why I wanted to come over this afternoon. I talked to your parents, and I think it's best to put you on medical leave for the next week, at least. Or until I think you're ready."

A rush of outrage spirals up straight from the pit of my stomach, pushing everything else aside.

"You can't do that."

Van pats the air in front of me like I'm a horse that needs soothing, which makes me want to spit at him. He can't sit there and say he's keeping me out of the pool and then expect me to be fucking calm.

"Brynn, you've been pushing your own limits for the last month, and I'm ashamed it took something like yesterday to make me see I've been letting you. It's no secret that you're one of the best swimmers I've trained, and working with you is an honor. You're strong, you're responsive, and you get your brain in the swim. Not a lot of people can do that, as you well know."

I'm blinking away tears, which is maddening. "So why keep me from doing it?"

"Because you obviously need some time off. And if I don't give it to you now, we'll both be sorry."

This isn't happening. I stand up, knees trembling and fists tight.

"I don't need anything except more training, obviously. If I'd been better prepared, yesterday wouldn't have happened at all. You think you've been pushing me, but it looks like you're wrong. I haven't been working hard enough. If you'd been paying attention to that instead of worrying so much about Grier and her bullshit, then maybe you would've been able to see it."

Van winces a little, but his voice stays steady. "I should've been paying a lot more attention to what was going on with Grier, actually. And you, for that matter. So maybe that means I need a bit of a break myself, too. The club owners might be right."

"What are you talking about?"

He shifts and clears his throat. "Let's just say that after yesterday—well, it's more than a reality check for me."

"What the main issue is, honey," Mom jumps in, "is that the way you've been doing things is obviously not working. We need to take some time, think about—"

"Did you see my time, Mom?" I shriek at her. "I think the way I've been doing things has been working pretty fucking dandy."

"Watch how you talk to your mother," Louis snaps. "And you ending up in the hospital is where you lose any kind of say in the matter, I'm afraid."

"You can't do this." I turn to Van. "I won't let you do this. You can't make me stop going to practice, and you can't keep me out of the pool. What about my scholarships? How'm I supposed to get those without State? This isn't about pushing myself, Van, this is about my life."

"You'll be fine at State," Van says, infuriatingly calm, "as long as you really rest. One week of that isn't going to kill you. Even in taper you've been pushing too hard, no matter what I've told you. You don't have to be first at State anyway in order to get everything you want."

"What I want," I growl, though it sounds more like a whine, "is to swim. I don't know why any of you can't get that."

Because I really am truly crying now, I rush away from them, flying up the stairs and slamming the door. I crash onto my bed and shove my face into my pillows, deep, so they won't hear the sobs that come out so hard and fierce, I don't know if I'll be able to make them stop.

44

I LIE THERE, LISTENING TO THEIR VOICES DOWNSTAIRS FOR A little while longer, until the door shuts and I hear Van's car drive away. I roll over on my back, staring at the ceiling, feeling the tears dry into crusty little rivers between my eyelashes and my ears. It doesn't matter what Van or Mom or Louis think. I'm not going to stop swimming. I've worked too hard. I need this too much.

I get up and go downstairs. I've gotten control of myself again. I know what I need to say.

"Mom, Louis." I stay on the stairwell, looking over the banister at them. "I know you're worried. It scared me, too, okay? I won't let it happen again. Things got out of hand, but now I know my limits. I know how to handle this, and I promise I won't overdo it. But you have to understand, I need this win."

Inexplicably, this makes Mom start to cry. I open my mouth to apologize, but she holds out her hand to stop me.

"Brynn, I'm sorry, but I need a minute before we discuss this any further."

My calm, sweet little act drops immediately away. "How much more is there to discuss, Mom? I don't understand what the big deal is. It's not like I'm vomiting blood or anything. I'm not—"

Louis looks up. "Just give your mom some space for a second, okay? The last twenty-four hours have been pretty intense."

I jut the inside of my elbows forward, showing him the taped-down cotton pads still covering my needle marks. "You think?"

"We know they have been for you, too," he says, rubbing Mom's back. "It's why we all need a minute to calm down."

This is infuriating. "Whatever. Fine. Let me know when you're done crying over one of the worst days in *my* life."

I head back to my room, because apparently Mom needs to take over the whole downstairs with how difficult this all is for her. For a minute I think about taking off down the street to Charlie's, but then I remember there'll be no going down the street to Charlie's ever again.

So I head to the bathroom instead, turning the shower on hard and hot.

. . .

As soon as I'm out of the shower, Mom calls up the stairs for me, saying she has something to say. I've had about as much of her as I can stand for a while, but it's not like there's anything else for me to do right now. Might as well let her say her piece so I can explain how she's wrong and then go back to doing what I want.

In the living room, Mom and Louis are next to each other on the couch. On the ottoman in front of them is a beat-up looking shoe box that Mom pushes toward me.

"What is this?" I scoff, the box giving me a strange feeling. "Some kind of stupid movie you saw on Oxygen?"

"Brynn, I asked you earlier about your tone."

"This isn't about you, Louis."

"Honey," Mom says, "it is about Louis because Louis loves you very much. And otherwise I don't think I would show you any of this."

There's a tingly feeling in my chest—a warning—but I snort and pick at the itchy edge of tape on my left arm. "What? Is there some brother out there I never knew about?"

Mom's quiet. When I look back up at her, the sad, apologetic expression on her face makes me know there's no long lost sibling or any other hokey crap from TV. Still, whatever she's about to say, I don't want to hear it.

"I've spent a lot of energy trying to preserve all your good memories of your dad without sharing the rest with you, Brynn. Maybe that's been a mistake; I don't know. But I feel like you're not giving me much of a choice right now. Louis and I knew you wouldn't listen much to either of us, but that you won't even listen to Van . . . I don't know how else to get through to you."

"Get through to me about what?"

She gestures toward the shoe box. "Take a look."

The level of how badly I do not want to open that box is completely irrational, so I make myself grab it and pull off the lid. But there's no mummified internal organs, or photos of Dad with another woman, or anything else like that in there. It's just a thin stack of the narrow little notebooks Dad carried in his back pocket.

"So?" I lift one to her. "What's so hard about showing me this?"

"Just look at what's in them, please."

I flip through the first one. Each page has a row of numbers—sometimes written in black pencil, sometimes in blue. Next to the numbers there are names and dates. Some of the names I recognize as belonging to guys from the station. A lot of them I don't know. At the bottom of each page there's a total, always circled. Sometimes with a lot of zeros.

I'm still confused.

"Your dad started keeping those books when he was sixteen

years old. I didn't have any idea about the extent of them until well after you were born."

"So? What is this?"

"You know we weren't able to give you a lot when you were growing up, and things were much worse for us after the accident. This is why."

I toss the notebook back into the box with the others. "Sorry. Still don't get it." But a creepy feeling has started to climb up my neck and around the back of my head. I'm remembering fights they had about money, Mom screaming, "You have to stop."

She takes in a breath and holds it, then lets it out slow. It's weird to see her do exactly what I do.

"When your dad died, he left you with an insurance policy, yes, but he also left you with this. His debts. Debts he owed to people because of his gambling problem. Some of them, thanks to the guys at the station, went away after he died. But there were a bunch of others that we couldn't get out of."

I can't help it. I laugh, nervous and thin.

She doesn't even blink. "He thought it was funny when I insisted he get help for it too, but I can tell you it was absolutely serious. Some nights, before he went into the program, I'd pace the kitchen, wondering if he wasn't betting away our house."

"Dad wasn't in any kind of program."

She nods once. "It was the summer you were nine.

Remember he was taking all those extra shifts? When he missed your birthday because of it?"

I remember Mom and Dad both explaining that he couldn't be there because of work, but then Mom took me to get my ears pierced and I had a sleepover with all my friends, so I hadn't much cared. It was the last good birthday I had before Dad died.

"You're saying Dad wasn't there because he was in some kind of rehab?"

"It was out-patient therapy, but yes. It's why he was gone so many evenings. Not that it did him much good, I'm afraid."

The part about Dad being gone so much doesn't really stick in my mind—I was used to him being away for several days at a time when he was on shift—but I do remember that summer: Dad stopped watching any sports on TV, and the guys didn't come over to grill and play cards. Dad also started lifting weights again in the garage and went on long runs. It was because he said he needed to be healthy.

The creepy feeling turns into a hot burn all over. Maybe he meant more than one thing by that.

"So, what you're telling me is that this whole time Dad had some . . . addiction, and that's why we never had any money? Why we had to move into that crappy apartment? Why I need a scholarship so bad for college?"

"What your mother's trying to say, Brynn—" Louis starts,

but there's no way I can hear anything from him about my dad right now.

"I'm sorry," I interrupt, voice full of contempt, "but I just don't see what this has to do with me and swimming. I don't know why you feel, on today of all days, like you suddenly need to dump this shit on me that you've been lying about for my entire life."

Mom's face fills with disappointment. And worse, pity.

"I understand you're angry," she says, calm and slow. "I was angry too. So angry, sometimes, I couldn't even look at you." She leans forward, rests her elbows on her knees, and holds my eyes with hers. "Brynn, you are an exceptionally gifted swimmer, and we are extremely proud of you. Your level of discipline and drive astounds me. Sometimes I don't know where you came from. But other times, like today, and how you aren't listening to any of us . . ."

She stops a second to swallow. I think she's going to start crying again, but she doesn't.

"Honey, we're not trying to take away your swimming or destroy your chances for the future. I'm not telling you about your dad's problem because I want to ruin any of the ways you think about him. He saved those two people—he saved more than those people. He was a hero. But he was also obsessed. Even when he'd dug himself so deep, he couldn't get out, when it was putting us all in jeopardy . . ."

She isn't looking at me anymore but searches the air with her eyes, seeing maybe the same things I see: beans and franks in a can for dinner. Dad hunched over that lawn mower that never worked, instead of paying to get it fixed. Going to garage sales for my back-to-school clothes. Chief Ramirez and all the guys from Dad's squad playing cards with him in the living room, laughing and cussing. Dad's portrait on his casket, surrounded by flowers.

"I'm telling you this now, because I think you need to hear that gambling was the main thing that mattered to your father. He was willing to let you, and me, and our whole life suffer for the sake of it. And I don't want you to suffer—not your social life or your education, and especially not your health—because of your own competitive fixation."

The room swirls then, and everything becomes unreal. It's enough. Too much. I stand up, disgust and disappointment blocking anything else I might feel.

"You just can't stand it that I'm the strong one, can you?" I shout at her. "That I was the one who made something of myself after he died, when all you did was dissolve into a pool of self-pity and resentment, shacking up with Louis so you wouldn't have to do anything anymore. You're a pathetic, jealous, weak little person, Mom, or else you wouldn't be doing this. People think I could get a gold medal with the right amount of work, and you want me to stop? You're gonna sit there and try to paint

Dad into some kind of monster so I'll stay home and sit there on the couch like you? Fuck all that. I don't care about Dad, or you, or anyone else. I care about winning at State, and getting into a good college, and actually finishing, like you never could! I care about getting the hell away from you is what I care about. Swimming is what I'm good at, Mom, and now you want to lay all this shit on me, saying I need to slow down? To take a break? Well, I'm not going to let you do that. Dad may not have had any discipline, but I do! I've got more strength than him, and certainly you, put together, and you just can't stand to watch it, can you? That's what this is about, nothing else."

I turn then and run back upstairs where I slam my bedroom door even louder than before. And though I hate her, and Dad, and Van, and Louis, and everyone for bringing me to this point, for the second time in not even twenty-four hours, I cry so hard, I think my lungs will explode.

45

AN HOUR LATER, MAYBE TWO, I'M STILL CURLED UP IN MY BED, staring at the wall. Though my vision is blurred from exhaustion and tears, in my mind I see all kinds of things swirling together like bubbles underwater.

I see Dad standing waist-deep in a lake we used to go to for firehouse picnics, me stretched out in front of him with his hands propping up my narrow back just under the surface. Teaching me how to float.

I see Mom bringing in the mail, tired from work, her eyes pouched underneath in a grayish purple. A glass of wine, and the TV, and me bringing in frozen dinners bought with coupons.

I see myself on the block, poised and ready. My shelves and bulletin board full of trophies and ribbons.

I see my girlfriends dropping away one by one.

I see Van leaning down over my lane, telling me what to do next.

I see Charlie wiping his eyes.

Kate telling me I'm an asshole.

Gavin whispering hotly what a bitch I am.

And I see Grier, too, standing there, shocked in the hallway light.

All these sacrifices, this discipline—they've been so nothing would get in the way of becoming the best at what I was built to do. So it isn't fair—it doesn't seem real—for Mom to step in and make me question it now.

Later—much later, though maybe not as late as it feels—Louis comes upstairs and knocks on my door.

"What is it?"

He opens it and leans in, carrying one of the dinner trays. On it is a plate with leftovers from our Italian feast Friday night.

"We didn't know if you were hungry," he apologizes.

"It's fine. You can just put it on my desk."

He picks his way around my laundry piles and my discarded gear bag leaking suits and towels, and puts the tray down.

"Hey, Louis?" I say, still prone on my bed, my arm tossed over my eyes.

I hear him pause between my desk and the door.

"Tell me what Van meant."

There's a quiet beat. "He meant he's worried about you. We all are."

I lean up on my elbows to look at him. "No, I mean that thing he said this afternoon. About a break. About the club."

He makes an uncomfortable sound out his nose.

"What did he mean about paying attention to Grier?"

"Look, Brynn, this is about you right now."

"I know it's about me. Van is my coach."

He moves from foot to foot and puts his hands in his pockets. "Nothing's been decided yet, okay? It's just a lot of angry e-mails from what I can tell right now."

"What are the parents saying, Louis? Quit beating around the bush."

He looks at me, hard. "Grier's parents are concerned. She . . . posted some things online . . . and there are some accusations going around that she was maybe compromised by one of the older teammates."

"You mean Gavin. That's why he and the other guys got switched to evening practice."

He clears his throat uncomfortably again. "No one's saying names. But the Hawkinses are pretty upset. They think that Van was . . . irresponsible. That there wasn't enough supervision."

"So they're going to fire him."

"That's not what anyone's saying right now."

"But that's what they think. Even if it isn't his fault."

I lie back down and shut my eyes under the weight of my arm. I know Grier's parents. I know they don't care, until suddenly they really, really do.

"You don't need to worry about all that right now," he says quietly. "Right now you need some rest."

"Yeah," I say with a laugh, though it comes out sad. "You know me. Worrying way too much about everyone else."

"Your mom's writing your teachers," he says. "You won't have to go to school until you're ready."

Sure, school.

Like that's the top thing I'm worried about fucking up.

When Louis leaves, I sit there in my bed, robotically forking lasagna into my mouth and staring into space. Today's pretty much been one of the worst in my life since Dad's accident, and talking to Louis just made me tired all over again. I don't want to think, but I know there won't be any swimming this off for a while. Mainly I want to lie down and fall asleep and never wake up. It's not that I want to die—I just don't want any of this.

Something keeps nagging at me though, while I scrape my plate clean and lick off the remnants of sauce and ricotta. About Van, and Gavin, and why he didn't come over on Thursday night.

So, since today's already been Mega Revelation Suck Day,

I go ahead and text him: hey i have a question. just one. okay?

I sit there, cross-legged, jiggling my knee, waiting. He still may not text me back. I could call, I guess, but I don't want to hear his voice, his breathing. It'd be too close. I could pull a Grier and text him relentlessly until he answers, but I think I've had enough crazy for today. I look at the clock—6:21. He could be anywhere. Having dinner, partying, hooking up with one of those sluts from the lake house. I might never hear from him again. Which, mostly, would be fine. The thought of him now—all the game-playing and secret grabs, him sneaking over here at night—feels stupid from this side of it. Even when I picture his hands on me, kissing him, I can't conjure up the same heat. All I feel, when I see him in my mind, is one big, deflated *Why?*

So it doesn't hurt—it isn't even annoying—when he finally texts back an hour and a half later: i don't really want to talk.

"Yeah, I don't either," I say to the air. "So let's get this over with."

jst want to knw if ur out of the club or not?

A minute, two, then: not for now. evening practice w/ littler kids, though they still may not think that's safe. if van's not coaching, i'll look at other options, anyway. not worth it.

I shut my eyes. If Van's not coaching . . . If. It's not a thing that's happening right now, but apparently it really is more than angry e-mails. I picture Van having to work with Troy, Linus, and Gavin all in one lane while encouraging the middle level at the same time. And Grier's mom, still squawking about how Gavin's some kind of predator.

Christ.

i'm sorry, I type. I don't know for which part right now, but I am. Sorry.

it's not your fault, he finally sends. but you can understand if—you know. it was fun though. i'll look for you in 2016.

Yeah, I can more than understand. The pit of my stomach feels hollow and raw even though I just ate. Gavin says it's not my fault, but there's no one else I have to blame right now for ruining my life and everyone else's.

46

MOM COMES IN TO CHECK ON ME BEFORE SHE LEAVES FOR work the next day. I've been awake for at least a half hour already, thinking. Thinking too many things I don't want to think.

She comes over, presses the back of her plump hand to my forehead. "How are you feeling?"

"I don't have a fever, Mom."

"I know you don't." She slides her hand down to my cheek. "Old habit."

Maybe before yesterday I would've told her I haven't been sick in years, say she hasn't done that in forever, and I haven't needed her to. But I don't really feel like saying anything to her right now. I turn my head away.

"You going to be okay here on your own?"

"I'm upset, Mom. Not suicidal."

I can feel her looking at me. "I know you're not. I'm just wondering if you need some company, maybe talk some more about yesterday."

Talk about yesterday? I have no idea how to start.

"You said what you had to say. I don't know what there is to talk about. Dad screwed everything up, and now it looks like I'm exactly like him. What is there to talk about?"

"Sounds like there's a lot to talk about, actually."

"Yeah, well, I'm not in the mood."

"Brynn—"

"Mom." My voice gets harsher. Her being in here, asking me, just makes it all worse, and I'm not going to cry again. Not today. "I said I don't want to talk right now, okay? You're going to be late."

She sighs and stands up. "I know it'll take some time, honey. And I want you to know I'm here when you're ready. I'm sorry I didn't tell you before. All I can do is be here now."

She waits, but I still don't feel like talking.

Eventually she goes, shutting the door behind her.

I stay in bed for hours, mostly doing nothing but watching a few videos, thinking, and drifting in and out of sleep. There haven't been any revelations, and I don't feel better about anything, but by one thirty I finally get up. I realize I haven't eaten much except the lasagna Louis brought in last night. Might as well eat some more, put some clothes on. Take another shower first. Act like a human.

Since there's nowhere I have to be, I spend a long time in the bathroom, letting the warm shower spray sluice down over me, feeling the hard muscles under my skin. Muscles that I've worked for, that can do anything. Anything except deal with all the shit in my head and figure out what my life will be like if I really have to take a break from swimming.

After I towel off, I put on a robe and go downstairs to make a sandwich. I bring it and a half a bag of popcorn up with me, climb back in bed with my computer. I don't know what I'm looking for. Maybe I'm just feeling sorry for myself, thinking about everything I've jeopardized, but the first thing I do is go to Charlie's pages.

There isn't a lot up. Like me, he's too busy to go online much. Maria's posted a few pictures from the Friday night dinners, but I'm not in any of them. Instead it's Charlie, Ethan, Nora, and Maria, plus some other people I don't really know, all smiling and making goofy faces, posing with chopsticks and holding up hands of cards. I look out the window toward Charlie's house. Maybe I should try to tell him I'm sorry, that he really was a good boyfriend and I didn't deserve him. Maybe he'd be willing to let me come over to try and explain. Maybe he would listen, help me sort out what's what, instead of all this mixed-up I feel.

But I also know that part of what I'd need to talk about would involve what ended up happening with Van and Gavin, and he sure as shit won't want to hear about that. Besides, sorry doesn't fix anything. Mom's said sorry a dozen times since yesterday, and it doesn't change how she was when Dad died or the fact that apparently he loved his gambling more than he loved me. Tears well up, thinking that plus seeing Charlie's smiling face on my screen. Charlie who didn't want me to prove anything. Charlie who kissed me in the only way that helped me sleep. Charlie, who made me laugh. Who thought I was a winner just by being around.

I close my eyes. I totally lost him, and I can't get him back. No matter how hard I work from now on, I'll never get anything back from the way it was before.

After a while of feeling sorry for myself, I go back to my screen so I can disconnect from Charlie. It's probably better that way. For him and for me. As I do, I realize I have fifteen different notifications, most of them tags from a page I follow, "What Should Swimmers Call Me," and one or two old things from Van or people on the team. The last one, from a week and a half ago, makes me pause though: *Kate Braught Wants to Connect.*

"No, she doesn't," I say out loud, laughing a little as I accept for the hell of it.

At first I'm not surprised by what's there, mainly posts about animals: lots of photos and quotes, plus links to Web cam videos surveying different animal babies—herons, hummingbirds, some rescued tigers in India. There are also several petitions, calls to support various animal rescue groups. I click through a bunch of photos of some weird collective called the Inman Park Squirrel Census, amazed. It looks like Kate is online almost all the time with this stuff, and she's connected to a ton of people. I'm stunned, seeing this supersocial online version of her. When she changed her status to "dating," for example, nearly eighty people sent up exclamation points and smiley faces, even the ones who seem to live in different countries. I liked Kate before, but now I am fascinated by the fact that her life is so much more complex and interesting than mine.

Turns out, she's not just social online, either, and not all her photos are of animals. There are five whole albums, all labeled Camp Callanwolde, from different years. In these are pictures of Kate in a canoe; Kate holding up charred marshmallows with two guys who have their arms around her shoulders; Kate participating in some kind of water balloon game; Kate smiling down from the back of a horse (and then several more of this horse, and Kate doing various things like combing it or cleaning its hooves); Kate doing cartwheels in a field with other girls; Kate hugging at least twenty different people.

I realize, looking at them, that I want to be in photos like this with Kate.

And then my chat screen flashes open: are you dying or something?

I laugh out loud, not believing. no I type back to her. just recuping.

i saw you were online. mr. woodham said you were in the hospital.

Then a second one: are you okay?

I'm amazed she's asking me, considering how mad she's been. Considering I was just looking at her stuff, missing her, and now she's here, just like that.

i guess i'm ok. And then, before I think too much about it: thx for checking. and i'm sorry.

She doesn't say anything back for a long time, and then: our drafts were due today. he's giving them back weds and then the finals are due mon.

i know, I type, though it's the first time I've thought of that paper in days. I've barely done the reading. I don't even have an outline.

you should check your messages. he's being pretty strict it sounds like.

I groan. Of course Woodham's being strict about it.

okay thx for the heads-up, I finish.

I wait for a while, but she doesn't say anything back.

Since everything else is pretty much shit today, I open a new tab and decide to face my in-box.

• • •

As soon as Mom and Louis are both home, I charge down the stairs, asking if they've checked their messages from my teachers. This is completely unfair, and I want them to see, too.

"Actually, it's pretty nice of him," Louis says, looking down through the bottom half of his reading glasses at his screen, taking in what Woodham's said about my paper, that at this point all he can do is give me an incomplete, and then expect the draft on Friday and my final within two weeks of the end of school. Chu wrote back to Mom too, about Enviro, saying I need to make up the end of the lab that I missed today, because part of the exam comes from it. Not to mention that I still have exams next week and need to finish those stupid Spanish flash cards.

Louis and Mom are hardly sympathetic when I complain I don't have enough time for all this, even if I do go back to school tomorrow.

"Seems like you had a fair amount of time, reading this," Louis says.

"I agree, honey," Mom adds. "It looks like you don't have a choice. It's either finish up this semester the way your teachers suggest, or it's summer school. I can't see that there's really another way."

Summer school. Which would mean absolutely no practice, because they make you sit there from seven a.m. to five p.m. for a solid four weeks, plus homework. And from the looks of it, I'd have to take more than one class, which might mean two sessions. But there's still State to prepare for. I have to nail National Cut there, if any of the rest of my college plans are going to happen. It doesn't matter what else is going on. There is no other option.

"Mom, are you forgetting that State's in two weeks? And after taking this week off like Van's making me do, I absolutely cannot afford to miss another one."

Louis looks at me, then at Mom.

I know what they're thinking.

"I'm taking this break, okay? I'll cram this week when I'm not at practice. But I'm not going to miss State. I can't. It's too big, and there's too much riding on it for me. If I can just get this one win, then next year I swear—"

But I stop. Because I hear myself. I don't even need to see Mom's face.

I collapse onto the couch, everything crashing in. "It's not like that," I say, my voice starting to tremble. "It isn't." But even I know better.

"I know it's not, honey," Mom says, soothing. "Because the thing about your dad was that he didn't know when to fold."

"So, what then?" I hit the couch in exasperation, my throat seizing up even more. "After all my hard work, it's no big deal? What am I supposed to think about that, huh, Mom? If none of it's going to matter, what the hell have I been doing all this time?"

She looks at me, her eyes and mouth soft with sympathy. "I think your future is going to turn out just fine, Brynn, because of your hard work. But that question also sounds like a good one to ask."

47

THE NEXT MORNING I STILL WAKE UP ACCORDING TO ROUTINE. I still do everything in order, still do my thing. Louis is still in the kitchen with his coffee. The only part that's different about any of it is me, and I'm not sure who that is right now.

There's no point in sitting at home for another few days, but being back at school right before the semester's over, when my whole life's been turned around, only hammers home the fact that I also have absolutely no friends. Yearbooks have apparently come out, and everyone is huddling over them in the halls or sharing phone pictures from all the extracurricular banquets that went on this weekend. Before, I wouldn't have cared, because I'd have been too focused on practice. Or Grier and I would have spent the weekend at her place, defacing everyone in her own yearbook and cracking each other up. Now, I have none of it.

The loneliness and understanding of what I've lost almost brings me to tears again. During lunch, I dodge the hall monitor and duck into the bathroom. I splash water on my face and then stand there, back against one of the stall dividers, staring hard into the mirror. I take in my sharp jawline, my hard body, everything about me nothing but fucking hard. And still—what? Still I'm here, like a weenie, crying in the bathroom.

I growl at myself in the mirror, make a fist, and punch my rock-hard pecs as fiercely as I can.

"You see that?" I shout, my voice echoing off the walls. "You see it? You made that. You made this whole thing, all by yourself. So what are you going to do with it now, huh? You going to turn pussy? Sit here and cry? Maybe your dad was a loser. Maybe he was. But he wouldn't be proud of this, and neither are you. So what the hell're you gonna do with yourself, huh? What're you gonna do?"

It shocks me, the answer that rings in my head: that I could just focus the same kind of energy on something else.

I get to Enviro early so that I can go over my schedule with Chu and find out when I can do the lab. She's irritated, but she's working with me. I even negotiate an extra day to finish the exam after school, since we can't do the lab until Thursday.

While I'm at Chu's desk, Kate comes in. Her brows go up a little bit in surprise when our eyes meet, but she quickly sits down. When I'm finished with Chu, the seat behind Kate is still open. She's not looking at me, and she probably doesn't care, but I move in behind her.

There isn't time to write notes or say anything, because now that my exams really matter, I have to pay attention. There's so much I've missed by not caring, by sleeping through class—for a minute it just seems pointless. The amount of studying I'll have to do is overwhelming. But as soon as the panic starts to seize me, without thinking I suck in my breath sharp, count to ten, and let it out slow. My blood stops whirling behind my eyes. My abs stay strong and tight, and the hardness of them, the way they hold steady, calms me down, same as it always does. So maybe I really can figure out how to be disciplined about the next steps too.

I look at the back of Kate's head, bent over her notes. I remember her smiling face in all those pictures, how she's subtly changed since she started dating Connor, and how fun it's been to watch. How much I admired her wide life yesterday, and how I want to be a part of it.

My grades aren't the only thing I could fix, if I worked at it.

So when class is over and Kate doesn't exactly wait for me to leave, but doesn't streak ahead of me either, I fall in step beside her.

"I thought you'd still be out" is the first thing she says.

"Yeah, well. Doesn't seem like I can afford to miss any-thing."

She slants her eyes at me. "What did Woodham say?"

"That I can have an extension. Take an incomplete. I still have to finish the paper, but he could've given me an F."

She makes a noncommittal noise.

"I deserve an F, I guess. I haven't really done the work."

There's another noise from her that I can't exactly translate, but it probably comes close to "I know." Initially it pisses me off, but it's true.

"Listen." I stop her in the hall, taking in a breath. "It doesn't fix anything, and I understand if you still hate me, but I do feel bad about what I did. It was selfish. I was treating you like —" In my head, I see it, how it was all just another competition for me to win. "Well, not like a friend. And I just want you to know that that's what I'd rather be."

She starts walking again, but she scoops her hand in the air for me to follow.

"We're going to be late," she mutters.

I keep quiet, focusing on keeping up with her sped-up walk. I think she won't say anything else before we get to Woodham's, and that that's the end of that, but then I hear her mutter, "Apologies don't —"

I grab on to it. "Apologies don't what?"

She sighs. We're at Woodham's door. Probably with only thirty seconds before the late bell rings.

"Apologies aren't necessarily supposed to fix things, is what I mean." She huffs up her bangs with a frustrated breath. "You can't make something you broke not broken just by apologizing."

She's glaring at me. I know I deserve it.

"But that isn't the point," she goes on, angry face shifting to something more thoughtful. "The point of an apology is to acknowledge that something happened. To recognize the harm done, so that maybe it's possible to, you know, put things back together and recover."

I think about Mom and all her *sorrys*. Realizing yesterday that I can never get Charlie back. How I owe Grier an apology too—Grier whom I suddenly miss in a way I didn't expect.

"Yeah," I say back to Kate. "But you break someone's plate or vase or whatever, even if you manage to glue it back, the cracks still show. And usually there's a chip or two you can never find. The original plate's still busted. It's pointless. You might as well just walk away, get a whole new plate."

"I don't know about pointless," she says, opening the door as the late bell rings, "but I do know—thanks in part to you, you big jerk—that the only thing you know if you don't try something, is that then absolutely nothing has the chance to improve."

• • •

So after class, after I talk to Woodham and tell him I appreciate and accept his offer, I apologize again to Kate, this time for real.

"Well, it was a pretty dickhead move," she says, moving us down the hall. "I might still be mad at you for a while."

"I know. Apparently, I don't know how not to be a dick." I say it funny, but it doesn't feel all the way like a joke.

"It's because you're an only kid." She nods seriously. "None of you know how to share. At this camp I go to, the whole first week, all the spoiled only kids are the ones with the most problems. It's why I'm glad I have a brother. Well, at least some of the time I'm glad. Siblings can suck sometimes, but they're also pretty useful."

We're almost to the pickup loop where Louis is waiting, but I don't want to stop talking.

"I saw that camp on your profile. What's the deal?"

She shrugs, a little embarrassed. "It's this three-week thing. I've been going since I was in sixth grade. It's really fun. And you learn a lot about yourself."

I nod, thinking. Three weeks is a long time. A long time to see what it's like having more in my life than the pool.

"I've already registered for first session," she goes on, watching my face carefully. "It fills up quick. But . . . there might be some openings later in the summer. My mom's on the advisory board, and I could probably make you a recommendation, if you were seriously interested. There's even a swimming concentration. The coaches are really good."

It doesn't matter to me if the coaches are any good. If I'm really not swimming with Van this summer—which feels insane, though maybe it's true—then, like Gavin, I'm not sure I want to be in the club at all. Maybe I'd take a pause, then rejoin the school team. Maybe it would help me and Charlie, maybe even Nora and Maria, go back to being friends.

"I have to think about it," I tell her, since we both have to head out. "But it sounds kind of cool."

48

INSTEAD OF GOING STRAIGHT HOME, I CONVINCE LOUIS TO take me by the pool. After talking to Kate and Gavin, now I need to talk to Van.

It's weird walking out there still in my school clothes instead of my suit and my cap. Weird watching everyone prep themselves for practice when I'm not joining in. Shyrah and several others look up and smile, glad to see I'm okay, but I don't stop to chat. I head straight past them all and knock on Van's office door.

For a second I think he's not in there—that maybe he really is on probation or fired or whatever Gavin and Louis have hinted at—but then the door opens, and he's there, clearly surprised.

"Didn't expect to see you. Come on in."

He clears off the chair next to his desk, which is covered in training manuals and a bunch of printed-out logic puzzles.

"I won't stay long." I remain standing. "I know practice is about to start. I'm glad you're here running it, at least. Louis told me about the Hawkinses."

"Well, it's not anything that's up for discussion if you understand, but we're working something out."

That he won't say so means it's bad, but if he isn't gone already, maybe it will end up okay. I want to say I'm sorry, but even after Kate's little speech, I know in this case it really won't help. The problem isn't that the pictures got posted—well, maybe a little it is. And that part is my fault. But I'm also sure that most of what Grier's parents are mad about is thinking their little princess would do anything so lewd in the first place. Not because of what it would mean about her, but what it would mean about them. So of course they would want to take it out on Van.

That she might get away with it makes my spine heat up, my joints tighten. I wish I could do something to make Grier lose out.

But as I let out my breath, I know that's all I've *been* doing. And now look.

"I just came by because I wanted to see what you'd say if I can't practice next week. If I have to miss State."

"What's the problem? Exams?"

I nod.

"Well"—he frowns a little, considering—"it'd be a setback for early college consideration. That's one thing we couldn't get around. And if you wanted to go for Olympic trials, we'd have to find a few out-of-town meets, maybe something seminational, but it could still be done. It's not ideal, but there are other meets where you could make National. Like I told you, you still have good chances for scholarships. Those won't be an issue, so long as you keep up your grade averages. You've always maintained the minimum to stay in the club, but if you need to buckle down for exams right now, absolutely that's what you should do."

I was hoping he'd help me figure out another way, but Van's always stressed that school is important. Even if it means forfeiting State.

"When you come back, though, we'll need to change your practice routine, work on some harder drills. More strength training too, just to give you an extra boost. I'd want to keep an eye on you, maybe regulate your diet, involve your parents so that we are sure you are getting the proper sleep. There's no question in my mind you can do it, if that's what you're asking. It'd take some hard work, but I already know that isn't your problem."

"Yeah," I say, pondering. More drills. Work with weights. A Van-approved eating regimen. A sleep diary signed by my parents. More sacrifice, more discipline.

And, after everything over the last few days, I'm not sure what for.

Van stands up and searches through the papers he moved from the chair a minute ago. "You set your mind to something, Brynn, and I know you can get it done."

"Yes, sir," I say, though I'm not really registering. "Thanks."

He smiles in a final way and gestures to the door. We walk together down the length of the pool, the smooth turquoise water mirroring our outlines on its surface. Before he turns and heads to the team, he shakes my hand, tells me to keep resting. Already he's distracted, ready to get another afternoon practice going, and a strange feeling ripples over me as I head out the doors. For the last six years, I've been pushing so hard to prove how much better I am, how I don't need anyone else. I've been mercilessly hard on myself, because I've thought I'm the only person I could count on to be strong. And the whole time, that's exactly what it's left me—alone.

As I step into the sunshine, into the clean outside air, I gulp in a big breath. For a moment I'm dizzied by this vicious cycle swirling around my head. I know that in order to break it, whatever I decide about the rest of this summer should be about life not just in the water, but out of it too. I know I want to see what that looks like, and not just because of what Mom told me about Dad. But because I do want friends like Kate who matter, and time to have fun, and maybe to not have to work so hard every day.

The idea of freedom like that, that ability to choose how I spend my time, is scary as all hell. I'm not sure I'll know how to do it. But as I blink away the whorls before my eyes, waving to Louis waiting in the car, I understand with a clarity that makes me smile—I really can do anything I want.

ACKNOWLEDGMENTS

Upon completion of another novel, the cup of gratitude in my heart overflows and soaks the floor. So many people to thank! So much to thank them for!

To Meredith Kaffel of DeFiore and Company: Thank you for the relentless hours of coaching, pushing, hand-holding, negotiating, encouraging, editing, and cheerleading you have done ever since we sealed our relationship. I honestly don't know how I did any of this without you in my life.

To Patrick Price, Editorial Director at Simon Pulse: Thank you for diving straight into this new relationship with me. Your personal pluck and keen-eyed precision made this novel as tight as Brynn's quads and as sleek as a wet seal. (And it was also fun!)

To everyone at Simon Pulse who worked on and cheered for this book: Thank you for all the efforts (both large and small) you make to get my writing out into the world. You all are a gold-medal team, and I am wicked grateful to have you.

To Lain Shakespeare, and Maggie and Leila Chirayath: Thank you enormously for spending so much time helping me with all the swimming research and making sure I understood all the fine details of life in the swim lane.

To my beloved benefactor, Scott Burland: Thank you for throwing both of us into all this head first and for keeping me and our home afloat while I figured out how to paddle. Thank you for comforting, cajoling, listening, encouraging, cheering, and understanding, and especially for sharing all that whiskey.

To Amy McClellan: Thank you for putting me through the drills necessary to come up with a plot here. You are the best specialty coach in this department, and I always look forward to you putting me through the wringer!

To my brilliant sister, Erika McCarthy: Thank you for your amazing insight into my writing, first of all, but also into Brynn and what her personal struggles and demons might be. Thank you for helping me understand the life of a high school swimmer, and for all the lessons you teach me about apologies and everything else.

To Anica Rissi: We did it in different ways this time, but I still thank you for helping me make this book. Thank you for looking at early pages, for listening and suggesting as a friend, and for all the training you've given me so far when it comes to writing novels.

To my cousin, Meg Howrey: Thank you for your inspiration, not just in terms of this book, but in writing, and life, as well.

To Monika Hermann Smith, Jenni King Barnes, Rachel Trousdale, Lisa Whittle, Stewart Haddock, Franklin Abbott,

Alice Murray, Eilis Gehele, Susie Evans, Amy Jurskis, Maria Barbo, Lauren McDevitt Sokal, Lei Lani Rogers, Jennifer Jabaley, and Jane Snyder: Thank you for helping me find the perfect name for Gavin!

Last and best, to my readers: Life without you is like a swimming pool with no water. Thank you for reading my books, for sharing them with your friends, and for making me feel like a winner every day.